Stripped to the Bone
Portraits of Syrian Women

Ghada Alatrash

Petra Books

Library and Archives Canada Cataloguing in Publication

Alatrash, Ghada, author
    Stripped to the bone : stories on Syrian women : their
courage and resilience / Ghada Alatrash.

Short stories.
Includes bibliographical references.
Issued in print and electronic formats.
ISBN 978-1-927032-46-6 (paperback)
ISBN 978-1-927032-47-3 (pdf)
ISBN 978-1-927032-48-0 (html)

1. Women--Syria--Fiction. 2. Syria--History--Civil War, 2011- --
Fiction. I. Title.

PS8601.L27S77 2016   C813'.6   C2016-902000-2
                                  C2016-902001-0

editing, design and layout
Petra Books
petrabooks.ca
Ottawa Ontario Canada
Managing editor Peter Geldart
Editor Danielle Aubrey

Cover photo David Salas

Choose the most beautiful flower for me...

Let it be more beautiful than the laughter of children ^

---

^ These lines are taken from the song, *Faraashah wa Zahrah*
(A Butterfly and a Flower), by Lebanese singer and composer
Zaki Nassif.

Please see the endnotes for all literary references.

Alatrash

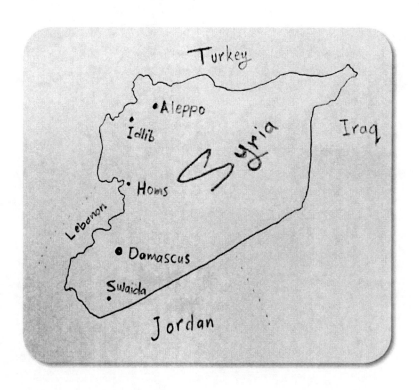

This map was sketched by a Syrian friend
who lives in exile today.

Alatrash

Dedication

To all the Syrian women in my life,
and to all women, of all colours of the rainbow,
who have taught me that being
a woman is the most beautiful existence of all.

To you, I dedicate every page of this book,
and to you, I also dedicate every heartbeat born,
every smile felt and every tear shed
while writing these pages.

Here is to being a woman…

Alatrash

Table of Contents

Preface

Postscript
Illustration credits
Index of first lines
Literary endnotes

Alatrash

Acknowledgements

Where do I begin?

It is overwhelming, and most humbling, to think of all the women and men who are part of my identity, and who are my inspiration behind the words in this book— the list is endless...but you know who you are, and this book came to be because of you.

The reflections, feedback, and comments of the following women have contributed great value to the making of this book: Selma Janbey, Lizette Deacon, Heather Janbay, Cathy Newsome, Raghda Azzam and Raeann Russell-Rivard—from the bottom of my heart, thank you.

To my professors: Thank you for teaching me to question a hegemonic discourse, to become a critical thinker, and to challenge that which has been deposited in our minds and is merely accepted and held as *beliefs* in our societies.

To Jabr (my beloved late father), Faiha, Gheath and Ghayth— thank you for always believing in me. To Ehsan— for the lesson we have learned from one another in the past twenty years of our lives. I wish you health and happiness. To Selma, Aamer and Marcel—I have learned from you more than you know; I love you.

— Ghada

Alatrash

Preface

These short stories are representations of my own opinion and an embodiment of my imagination. They spring from my personal experiences in life. I represent no one but myself. I predict that some of you might agree with my opinions, and I can see others shaking their heads in utter disapproval.

My stories embody my views and feelings on the many mundane acts that are carried out in our lives either robotically, and simply not for discussion, or have not yet been questioned. I am not waging war nor am I calling for a revolution; I am simply reflecting on life from my own lens as a Syrian-Canadian woman, and sharing that which I have seen and learned.

I am writing to question and to challenge a narrative that has dominated our lives for the past hundreds of years, and that has imprisoned our ability to think freely, confining our intellect within a very narrow box.

I wish for you and I to think together outside this man-made box, and to unleash our minds into the vast, free, and unlabeled horizons, or perhaps, as in the words of the Indian writer, philosopher and medical doctor Deepak Chopra: "instead of thinking outside of the box, get rid of the box." [B]

Perhaps writing these stories has been a way of clearing my mind and heart; and perhaps it has been my tool for re-constructing a scattered self.

And perhaps a story was written with the desire to amplify a dear woman's voice, and to shed light on the hurdles and roadblocks she had faced during her personal walk in life. However, I wholeheartedly ask of my readers not to generalize.

None of my stories are a representation of an entire culture or a sect. They are one story of one woman or one man, one flower or one thorn, in a colourful field that extends to the borders of the earth. Zahrah's circumstances, for example, are not a representation of all Druze women, nor are Mayyada's and Reem's of all Muslim women.

While reading, you may smell the aroma of jasmine in some of my pages and perhaps the scent of cigarettes in others. You may find a forgotten garment or a silver earring left behind under a duvet cover in a love scene. Or perhaps you will find a piece of wisdom hidden in between words in a dark prison cell or in a black Samsonite suitcase. Whatever it is that you find, it will ultimately also be a piece of my heart or perhaps one borrowed from someone else's heart, and so I hope that you handle it with care for what comes from the heart is always raw and stripped to the bone.

... continued in the *Postscript*

Stripped to the Bone

Alatrash

The poet Nizar Qabbani

I have a friend, a physician, who has once confessed to me that smoking a few puffs of marijuana is the best brain stimulant before embarking on medical research. I am not a marijuana smoker; the shisha[1], alongside a few glasses of wine, has been the extent of my narcotic adventures.

However, I have found substitutes to marijuana that I also inhale each time I sit to write; my substitutes are a selection of deliciously intoxicating poets who come with different flavours, all of which are quite stimulating to the cells of my mind and body.

One of those stimulants happens to be Syrian poet Nizar Qabbani. If you haven't read him, believe me when I say that you have missed out on something very special, something that dizzies the mind and the body. Ask other Syrian women about him, or any woman who has read him for that matter, regardless of nationality! If you are a man, I lovingly suggest you read his teachings on women and on love for you are bound, without a doubt, to find hidden treasures and precious advice in the pages of his poetry books.

So, here is a puff for you with a Nizarian flavour (so that we may begin this book on the same note and in the same mood).

---

[1] *Shisha* is also called hookah, water pipe, or *narghile.* The word comes from the Persian word for glass. The term *shisha* is primarily used for water pipes in Egypt. Westerners may erroneously refer to the tobacco smoked from a water pipe as "shisha", since in the Middle East it is acceptable to request a "flavoured shisha"— a hookah with flavoured tobacco.

Ablution
with Rose Water and Jasmine

Nizar Qabbani ^C

My voice rings out this time from Damascus.
It rings out from the house of my mother and father.

In Damascus, the geography of my body changes;
my blood cells become green
and my alphabet becomes green.

In Damascus, a new mouth sprouts from my mouth,
a new voice sprouts from my voice;
and my fingers become a tribe of fingers.
I return to Damascus
riding on the back of a cloud
riding the two most beautiful horses in life—
the horse of passion
and the horse of poetry.
I return after sixty years
in search of my umbilical cord,

... I return to the womb in which I was formed
and to the first woman who taught me
the geography of love
and the geography of women.
I return after my pieces have been scattered
in all continents,
and my cough dispersed in all hotels;

for since my mother's laurel-soap scented bed sheets,
I have found no bed on which to sleep.
...I submerge myself in the Bzurriya Market
and I delve into clouds of spices and cloves,
of cinnamon,
anise,
and rose water
again and again.

And I forget while in the herbal market
all of what was manufactured by
Nina Ricci and Coco Chanel.
What has Damascus done to me?
How is it that this city
could transform my education
and my aesthetic taste?

For the ringing of cups of liquorices
has made me forget
the piano concerto of Rachmaninoff.

How the gardens of Damascus have transformed me
into becoming the first conductor in the world
leading an orchestra
of willow trees!

... I remember the Damascene houses
with their copper door knobs,
their ceilings embroidered with glazed tiles,
and their interior courtyards
resembling the descriptions of heaven.

7

The Damascene house
is beyond architectural text.
The architecture of our homes

is based on an emotional foundation,
for every house leans on the hip of another
and every balcony
extends its hand to another facing it.
Damascene houses are enamored houses
that exchange visits
secretly at night.

When I was a diplomat in Britain,
thirty years ago,
my mother would send me letters
with the arrival of Spring.
Inside each letter
was a bundle of tarragon.
The English were suspicious of my letters,
and so they took them to the laboratory,
examined them under laser rays,
and turned them over to Scotland Yard.
But as they gradually became weary
of me and of my tarragon,
they asked,
'Tell us, by God!
What is the name of this magical herb
that has dizzied us?
Is it a talisman?
Is it medicine?
Or is it a secret code?

What is it called in English?'
I replied:

'It's difficult for me to explain
for tarragon is a language
that only the gardens of Damascus speak.
It is our sacred herb
and
our perfumed eloquence.

And, had your great poet Shakespeare
known of tarragon,
his plays would have been better.

In short,
my mother is a very kind woman
who loves me very much,
and whenever she misses me,
she sends me a bouquet of tarragon.
To her, tarragon happens to be
the emotional equivalent
for ḥabeeby, 'my beloved'. [2]

... As the English did not understand
one word of my poetic argument,
they gave me back my tarragon
and closed the investigation.

---

[2] *Ḥabeeby* is Arabic for the masculine form of My Beloved.

Alatrash

Story 1

ZAHRAH

The Art Teacher

Youssef Abdul Samad [D]

...
For I,
I worship pomegranate trees,
under whose shade
I used to sleep

...
While I plucked them off,
their fire burned me,
and the burn scars still remain
after the years...

...
Once,
I drew a lemon tree on paper,
and from its radiance,
its leaves almost budded.
I drew two pomegranates of fire,
and I tasted them—
You who dwells in fire,
believe it when they say
that fire can be such delight.

I still call to mind
their nudity
and I muse over them,
for the harvester is: lustful.

How is it
that pomegranate seasons
never come to an end,
nor does their
overflowing blood
ever burst?

And how is it
that they do not gush
while we eat them?
And how is it that
we do not see their fire
as they burn?

Alatrash

ZAHRAH

Naked, she stood across from the mirror admiring her breasts. They were perfectly round, swollen like two pome-granates. No man had ever touched or felt their perfection. "What a pity!" she lamented.

She stroked them gently, yearning to feel that sensation she had read about in novels and seen in movies—a feeling that is said to be triggered by a man's touch and is always accompanied by a moaning sound voiced by Hollywood actresses. But the touch of her fingers was not enough to arouse any moans. She tried but to no avail. She had realized that she needed a man's touch, but where was this man and would he ever show up?

Zahrah's [3] favourite time of the day was during the late evening hours, after all the chores were finished and after her father had gone to sleep. Ever since the uprising in Syria, the electricity was out in the evenings. Darkness injected a great dose of fear into the hearts of people, and instead of visiting one another as had always been the custom, they now chose to stay home and lock not only their doors but also every window of their homes. And so it was that Zahrah

---

[3]   *Zahrah* is Arabic for Blossom, a flower, splendour, beauty. It is also used as a feminine name.

found companionship in American movies and awaited the night hours with what had become a notable addiction, not only for the movies but also for the feelings they stirred in her thirsty body.

Zahrah craved to feel. With feelings came beauty, and there was nothing wrong with being addicted to beauty. She loved to dream. There was nothing wrong with dreaming. She thought of a quote by Rumi [4]: "Close your eyes. Fall in love. Stay there."

So, she closed her eyes and dreamt.

Only four years ago, before the Syrian crisis enveloped the country with its fires of hell, Zahrah's town, a suburb on the outskirts of Damascus, pulsated with noise and music. The streets were crowded with young men driving their waxed cars, their hair gelled suavely, speakers amplified, windows rolled down, and sugared comments flying from their flirtatious mouths and landing in the ears and hearts of the smiling young women standing by.

But those days are long gone. The sound of the music was now replaced by the bombing and shelling, the songs by news, and young men were no longer young but had aged hundreds of years with their minds occupied, not on girls, but on whether or not their families had enough food to eat and enough money to buy diesel for their heating tanks.

Yet, despite the enveloping darkness, gloom, and contagious despair, Zahrah was nonetheless able to find her escape through a secret tunnel that carried her into a world of magic and fairytales. While the electricity was on for a few hours

---

[4]   Jalāl ad-Dīn Muhammad Rūmī, and more popularly known as Rumi was a 13th-century Persian poet, jurist, Islamic scholar, theologian, and Sufi mystic.

during the day, Zahrah would make certain that her computer was plugged in and her battery recharged for the night hours. She had become aware of the fact that she found herself contentedly awaiting the outages so that she could sneak into her bed and select another Arabic-subtitled Hollywood movie to accompany her during the lonely nights.

The shop next door, Abu Fadi's, was the hottest store on the block as young men and women patiently awaited their copies of the latest Hollywood movies. They left their own DVDs in the shop early in the morning while on their way to school or work, marked with their names, and came back to pick them up by the end of the day or the next day, depending on the electricity and whether or not Abu Fadi was able to copy the movies before the outages.

Those movies were not only movies but were like intoxicating cocktails with which to quench their thirsty hearts, minds, and their starved appetites. Those movies were their plane tickets to the West and their dreams virtually manifested and only for a few Syrian pounds, cheaper than the cost of a loaf of bread these days.

Zahrah was 36, a late age for marriage as per the ratings of the Syrian system, for thirty was pushing it and 36 was beyond.

She had many movies to choose from; today, she decided on *The Bodyguard* with Whitney Houston, for she had often heard about how romantic it was but had not yet seen it.

The movie had her mind spinning in circles as she thought of the polar extremes of the world in which she lived. She was Druze [5], and as is the case with many religious sects, intermarriages were discouraged and socially off-limits. Hence her choices were limited to men who were born Druze, and, moreover, whose father, mother, and grand-parents were also preferably Druze.

Whitney Houston was as black as they came and Kevin Costner was as white as they were made. For the two to fall in love and for the Western community to embrace the union of this dichotomy was a phenomenon saturated with beauty and open-mindedness. It was definitely an admirable and humane characteristic.

Was this the case in the whole of the U.S., or was it only in Hollywood, she wondered. She turned over the DVD cover and read that the movie was released in 1992.

Yet only a few days earlier, she had heard the news about the Ferguson shooting of unarmed Michael Brown by a white police officer, and of the racial tension and civil unrest that was sparked as a result in the streets of the United States of America.

She realized that nowhere is utopic, but despite all, she admired the statement made by this movie of progressive-ness and acceptance. After all, the president of the United States of America is none other than a black man!

She thought of her own society, of the divisiveness that was caused by culture, religion, and out-dated creeds. There were labels and tags on everyone: "Christian" or "Muslim",

---

[5] *Druze* are a community representing a sect of Islam and they reside in Syria, Lebanon, Jordan, Palestine and the Golan territory. The Druze population is estimated to be one million people.

"Sunni" or "Shia", "Druze" or "Sunni", and today "pro" or "anti" (regime). But why couldn't the labels have simply been humane or inhumane, she thought to herself, and if humans were to be stripped to the core, to the bone, would the colour of their skins make any difference after all?

She anticipated the love scenes in movies. The moment that the hero and heroine kissed always sent an electrical wave through her body, from head to toe. It was a most mysterious and sensual sensation, one that brought her closer to God as she contemplated His most complex creation of the human body. How could a kiss on a TV screen ignite such a feeling, she thought to herself.

She recalled the pomegranates on her body, felt them as she watched Kevin and Whitney in an embrace, and delighted in the pleasure of a tingling sensation that travelled through her body and sent her into deep slumber.

"Get a fruit tray and coffee ready *ḥabeebty* ⁶ Zahrah. A young man from a good family is coming to see you tonight," said Zahrah's father in a voice that was as gentle as the kiss he planted on her forehead.

Zahrah loved her father very much. She knew, wholeheartedly and without a particle of a doubt, that he only had her best interests at heart. But she was also aware of the fact

⁶   *Ḥabeebty* is Arabic for the feminine form of My Beloved, or My Dear.

that her father's traditions of fifty years ago were no longer an adequate fit within the fast-changing world in which she now lived. Her hope for change came from the fact that many of her friends' parents, who were just as Druze, had slowly but surely shed the old and began to not only accept but also embrace the new.

And as much as she loved her father, she despised the idea of a potential suitor coming to "see her". It simply defied all of her beliefs and principles. The contradiction between what she lived and what she preached to her young female students was as polar in extremes as the earth and sky. There was nothing more difficult than acting against one's convictions and beliefs, but she had no other choice. A stranger was coming to visit and inspect her, and would then decide on whether or not she met his standards of beauty. It all begins with beauty, like in the process of picking a fruit before tasting it, where one feels how ripe it has become, turns it over to make certain it doesn't have any damage, perhaps smells it, and then tastes it.

If she were a fruit, she wondered, which one would she have wished to resemble? She examined each fruit while washing it and compared it to her body. She was definitely on the plum side, so perhaps a round plum best resembled her. However, her breasts looked like pomegranates. If she were proud of one thing, it would be the roundness of her breasts, so perfect that a Hollywood actress surely would have been envious. She thought of the other women she knew. Some had breasts that resembled apricots, round like hers but not quite as full and voluptuous as pomegranates. Some had lemon-like breasts, more on the oval side. She knew of a girl down the street whose breasts looked like cantaloupes, but she did not envy her at all as they looked too large to carry on her body, to the point of discomfort. She certainly didn't wish to carry around cantaloupes all day long. She was very content with her pair of pomegranates.

He had a silver moustache. She couldn't bear the thought of one day feeling his moustache on her breasts. He was not young, as implied by her father. Young, in her eyes, and considering her age, was early 40s to mid-50s.

However, she reasoned, there were always exceptions to the rule. She recalled a friend of her mother's who was married at 16 to a 52-year-old man. Their marriage to this date was the talk of the town. It was said that this man adored his young wife and worshipped the ground that touched the soles of her feet. One of the rumours was that before she went to sleep, he would massage her feet with oil and lotions and would kiss every toe in gratitude for his generous fate.

The story of this woman was one that often surfaced in the gatherings of the neighbourhood, and it always caught Zahrah's full attention and captivated her as if it were her first time to hear it. The woman's name was Sham. After her marriage, Sham immigrated with her husband to the U.S. and has since lived a life envied by all her married friends. She travelled the world. She also received an education and was granted a university degree. She had come from a forgotten village in Syria. She had never attended school, nor had she ever stepped outside the borders of her little town.

Zahrah often thought about this woman and how she could have ended up like many of the other neighbours, a housewife, bearing children and living life's successes and failures through the identities of her children. But instead,

Sham was presented with wings to fly, perhaps by a husband, or more realistically, by a generous fate. She soared the skies with her wings and crossed endless borders. She smelled the aroma of new worldly flowers and gathered their seeds to plant back in the fertile grounds of her homeland. The people of the neighbourhood awaited her return every summer, as did the flowers in their flowerbeds, for there was nothing more beautiful than new added colours and fragrances to a garden.

Zahrah would not have minded such a fate. Indeed, there was great mystery in whom fate chose as deserving or undeserving of a happy life.

However, as is the case with everything in life, all things come to an end. The husband was diagnosed with a terminal illness and died in his late seventies leaving his wife widowed in her mid-40s. Sham was a flower that had bloomed in a garden watered by love, adoration, and respect. It had been eleven years since his passing, yet Sham remains widowed and single, as it is said that she believes no one worthy or capable of walking in the empty and sacred shoes of her late husband. She also didn't trust that fate would be generous twice in one lifetime. Zahrah agreed.

Zahrah guessed that the man who sat across from her must have been in his early 60s. He didn't possess any special characteristics that could have potentially rounded down the figure. She watched as one of his hands hovered over the fruit tray, deciding on which fruit to land. Her late mother taught her to choose the best of fruit for their visitors and to place the ripest and roundest on top.

As she saw his hand snatch the pomegranates, she began

to sweat. Her head began to pound while her eyes followed the knife in his hands as it dug into the skin of the fruit. She felt a sharp pain in her nipples and moaned. Unaware of the torture he was causing her, he proceeded to remove the crown and carefully outlined the outer skin of the pomegranate separating it into two halves, making certain that he didn't cut too deep. He then placed the knife on the tray, and with the pomegranate in his two hands, he pressed at the centre dividing it into separate parts. Finally, while her father was trying to carry on a conversation with him, the bachelor turned one of the halves over his bowl and began hammering the outer skin of the pomegranate with a spoon, watching the shy pink seeds fall into the plate.

A few drops of the flying pomegranate juice landed on his white shirt. Her mother had also taught her that the best way to remove a pomegranate stain was to immediately soak the fabric in cold water. She did not care enough about the shirt, or the man, to share her mother's sacred advice. With a smile below his now red-spotted white moustache, he handed the plate with the fallen seeds to Zahrah and said, "For you".

Zahrah glanced at her also smiling father and then quickly looked down at the plate of seeds in her hands, straining to hide a smile that was threatening to explode into laughter. Just then, the electricity was cut off, and Zahrah was grateful for a darkness behind which she could hide her smile.

What has happened to Zahrah, you ask? Well, not surprisingly, she remains single. She has received her Ph. D. in English Literature from the University of Damascus. Watching movies at night helped with improving her English accent as well.

Her fate had also teasingly introduced her to the man of her dreams, Qusay [7]. He was everything she had ever dreamt of: open-minded, charming, romantic, wise, experienced, educated, worldly, and without a silver moustache; but alas, he was Christian, a little too far! So, she has not had the courage to break her father's heart and defy her father's, grandfather's, or great-grandfather's traditions.

And, as happens to be the case with many other Syrian women, her story with Qusay will carry on until he either decides to pursue a more promising relationship, or until she finds a suitor who fits within the boundaries of her father's definition of what is acceptable, but also, and most importantly, of what she has come to deem acceptable. In the meantime, she has decided that she remains unmarried and barren rather than to be married to a man whom she does not love.

Zahrah continues to be grateful, every morning, for her God-given gift of pomegranates.

---

[7]   *Qusay* is a masculine name and it is Arabic for He Who is a Little Far Away.

Stripped to the Bone

Alatrash

Story 2

REEM
&
MAYYADA

When I am overcome by weakness

Najat Abdul Samad [E]

When I am overcome with weakness, I bandage my
heart with Syrian women's patience in adversities.

I bandage it with the upright posture of a Syrian
woman who is not bent by bereavement, poverty, or
displacement as she rises from the banquets of death
and carries on shepherding life's rituals. She prepares
for a creeping, ravenous winter and gathers the heavy
firewood branches, stick by stick from the frigid
wilderness. She does not cut a tree, does not steal,
does not surrender her soul to weariness, does not ask
anyone's charity, does not fold with the load, and
does not yield midway.

…

I bandage it with the steadiness of a child's steps in
the snow of a refugee camp, a child wearing a small
black shoe on one foot and a large blue sandal on the
other, wandering off and singing to butterflies flying
in the sunny skies, butterflies and skies seen only by
his eyes.

I bandage it with December's frozen tree roots, trees
that have sworn to blossom in March or April.

I bandage it with the voice of reason that was not
affected by a proximate desolation.

I bandage it with veins whose warm blood has not yet
been spilled on the surface of our sacred soil.

I bandage it with what was entrusted by our martyrs,
with the conscience of the living,
and with the image of a beautiful homeland
envisioned by the eyes of the poor.
...

Alatrash

REEM
&
MAYYADA

Blindfolded, they led her by the hair. She kept her head tilted in front of the rest of her body so that the pain would lessen. She had never been in a prison before; she had only heard of the torture and seen it in movies.

Everything was surreal.

"You fucking prostitute," a man's voice barked in her ears as he dragged towards the prison cell. "Join the other prostitutes and fuck each other until one of us comes and fucks you."

He jerked the blindfold off her eyes, pushed her inward, and slammed the door behind her.

She squinted. It took a few minutes for her to make out her surroundings. She was in between four walls. The room was small and the air was suffocating. There was a dim light that came from the cracks of the metal door. Otherwise, there was no light.

She was placed in the "Scorpions" wing. She had heard that it was the worst of all prison cells. She wondered if it was called so because it housed scorpions. Her biggest phobia was cockroaches. She despised cockroaches, but today she hoped for cockroaches rather than scorpions.

A woman's voice came from within the darkness, "Sit down; you will have plenty of time to try to understand, but for now, just sit my dear. Take advantage of the moments when you can sit. I am sure you've had a long day."

Reem [8] narrowed her eyes to better see in the dark, looking for the voice that was coming from the other corner. She saw a silhouette of a woman, sitting on the floor with her knees pulled to her chest. She wore a sweater on her hair.

"My name is Mayyada [9]. What is your name?" asked the prisoner.

"Reem," she answered as she gradually slid against the wall and onto the floor.

There was a long period of silence. Reem fell asleep.

She was awakened by the screaming noises from a nearby cell. There were pleas, shrieks, and deafening screams, "For God's sake, for Mohammad's sake, for the sake of Al-Kaaba." [10]

"What are they doing to her?" screamed Reem, her body shivering.

Mayyada remained silent.

"Have they done that to you too?"

---

[8] *Reem* is Arabic for White Antelope, addax. It is used as a feminine name.

[9] *Mayyada* is Arabic adjective for A Female Who Sways or moves rhythmically from side to side. It is used as a feminine name.

[10] *Al-Kaaba* is the most sacred site in Islam, and is a cuboid building at the centre of Islam's most sacred mosque, Al-Masjid al-Haram in Mecca, Saudi Arabia. One of the five pillars of Islam requires every Muslim, who is able to do so, to perform the hajj pilgrimage at least once in their lifetime which includes a series of rituals, one of which is to walk counter-clockwise seven times around Al-Kaaba. When outside Mecca, a Muslim is to face the direction of Al-Kaaba in Mecca while performing a prayer.

There was no reply.

"Have they tortured you? I want to know. Will they torture me?"

"I don't know."

Reem screamed, "Have they tortured you?"

"Keep your voice down!"

"What did they do to you?"

"Stop. It's not a story to tell. Please stop."

There was silence once again, interrupted by more shrill screams sending cold chills down Reem's spine. She had never felt as scared in her life. There was horror in hearing the screams, one that she would find more horrifying than physical torture.

"Believe it or not ... I would rather...be here than where... I came from," expressed Mayyada in fragments of sentences that were squeezed into the silences between the screams.

Reem looked into Mayyada's expressionless eyes. They were blue, as blue as the sky that she had been standing under earlier in the day.

Mayyada inserted her hands into her shirt and felt the scarred skin on her back, "At least here I don't have to be tortured by my own brother. That bastard has left marks all over my entire body."

Reem was surprised by Mayyada's abrupt openness. People were afraid to be open these days, for even the walls were not trustworthy. She reckoned that she must have been in silence for so long that the words couldn't stay put any more. She also noticed that there was no clock on the walls, and her watch had been taken away upon reaching the prison cell. This must be another form of psychological torture, for one is surely to lose one's mind amidst the noise of shrill screams, the obscurity of darkness, the oblivion of timelessness, and the haunting thoughts of scorpions possibly creeping in from under the prison door.

The screams were still heard, but they were growing weaker, running out of breath.

"Why?" Mayyada carried on, asking herself the question on behalf of a terrified Reem, "Because he caught me without the *niqab* [11] on my face. That bastard. He decided to make my salvation his responsibility. Have you ever heard of a sister hating her own brother?" And without waiting for a reply, she continued, "Well, I do. I hate my brother with all my heart!" She then sat silent, with a trace of a smile that expressed her sense of relief at being able to announce her hatred and say the words.

Mayyada's brother was 25 years old. He was younger than she was but had the authority, as the only man of the house after the passing of his father, to dictate the rules as he interpreted them, one of which was for Mayyada to wear a niqab and to cover her face which, according to him, was also considered *awrah* [12].

Every few weeks, she would arrange with her best friend, Ghazal [13], to pass by her home in her brother's absence and to

---

[11] *Niqab* is a cloth that is worn to cover the face of a woman as part of Muslim religious beliefs. Many Muslim women wear the niqab; however, many others do not.

[12] The Hans Wehr Dictionary of Modern Arabic defines awrah or aura as "defectiveness, faultiness, deficiency, imperfection, pudendum, genitals; weakness, weak spot". In Islam, awrah is an expression used to refer to specific body parts that should be covered. A man's awrah is from his navel to his knees. A woman's awrah is her entire body excluding her face and hands; however, for some Muslims, the face of a woman is also considered awrah.

[13] *Ghazal* means to display amorous behaviour, court, woo, flirt, philander. The noun means: flirt, flirtation, dalliance; words of

beg her mother's permission to leave the house and visit surrounding shops. And, as happens to be the case with all mothers, her mother also had a soft heart, and it only took a few words, smiles, and kisses before she would grant her daughter consent to leave the house for a few hours, while asking that "God may keep close watch over her".

Each time she set foot on the front door steps of her home, Mayyada nervously covered her face with the black niqab and re-adjusted her black *abaya* [14] making certain that all the outlines and curves of her feminine figure were covered so that she did not tempt a man's eyes to lust over her body.

Syrian women were created beautifully. They were curvy and wide at the hips. There was nothing linear in the geography of their bodies; their peaks soared into heavenly skies and their dazzling valleys had endless depths; they were a world without an end. Indeed, God's creation of Syrian women reflected the most refined of palates.

Mayyada didn't mind the black concealment for it was but a small price she paid in order to breath the fresh air outside of her asphyxiating home, even if God's clean air had to be filtered through her niqab. In her brother's eyes, a *niqab* shielded a woman's body and soul from men's dirty thoughts and sexual desires, and shielded both parties from

---

love, cooing of lovers; love poetry, erotic poetry. Ghazal is also used as a feminine name.

[14] *Abaya* is Arabic for Cloak. Essentially it is a loose over-garment or a robe-like dress.

sexual yearnings and temptations.

Nevertheless, she was elated to be out in the open and fresh air. She and Ghazal were free and bound for the mall. They hopped into the taxi and asked the driver to take them to Town Centre, a modern mall boasting the latest Western fashions. The Cham City Centre [15] was nothing to compare with *Souq Al-Hamidiyah* [16] which boasted hundreds of shops that bustled with Syrian merchandise of mosaics and wood art works, iron and copperware engraved with Arabic art calligraphy, flamboyant fabrics of silk and velvet, and everything else Syrian-made. Each shop leaned on the back of another in a tunnel-like building with an ornate iron dome-like ceiling that continues to stand today in its full elegance. Mayyada's favourite shop in the *Souq* was the Bakdash Ice Cream Parlour, which made the best local Syrian ice cream, hand pounded in front of its customers and smothered in pistachios.

Yet as enchanting as it was to visit the old *souqs*, there was also an alluring sense to the ambience of modern Western-style malls with posters hanging on windows of shops boasting tall blonde European models, less curvaceous than Syrian females, but piercingly seductive with their nearly transparent light-coloured eyes. Italian and French brands like Benetton and Elle attracted Syrian women of all

---

[15] *Cham City Centre* is a modern mall located in the heart of Damascus with 3 stories of retail shops, dining, and entertainment outlets.

[16] *Souq Al-Hamidiyah* is a large central market in Syria, located inside the old walled city of Damascus next to the Citadel and built in two stages —in 1780 and in 1884. It is one of the treasures featured in BBC's travel documentary "Around the World in 80 Treasures. "

ages as they looked for contemporary styles and bold fashion statements to express their identities in a changing Syrian landscape.

As Mayyada and Ghazal passed through the sliding doors of the main entrance of the Cham City Centre, Ghazal convinced Mayyada to lift the niqab off her face. With trembling hands, she did. She felt the eyes of those around her staring and panicked. Ghazal felt her fear and spiritedly comforted her, "They're looking at your magical blue eyes, crazy! What a shame it is that you have to hide your magnificent God-given beauty."

Mayyada thought about Ghazal's words. She contemplated God's thought process as he had decided to make blue eyes, and whether or not he had intended for them to be covered with a niqab; why would He have made them in the first place if they were to be covered?

Gradually, she acquiesced and pushed her fears aside. During those few hours, she lived the most beautiful moments of her life. She admired the Western merchandise. The colour of the red leather boots behind the glass seemed brighter and more cheerful without the niqab in front of her eyes. She gazed at the perfect figures of the female mannequins behind the windows and thought of her own body. She thought of her curves and was certain that she would have been chosen as a model had her fate granted her different circumstances.

Her favourite shop was one that displayed wedding dresses embroidered with white pearls and diamonds. Everything in it was spectacular.

"We would like to try on one of your wedding dresses," Ghazal said to the handsome young Syrian merchant, also with blue eyes, "You see, my friend is getting married."

Mayyada stood speechless at her friend's words and she began to quietly recite a *Sura*[17] from the Koran in repentance for her friend's lies.

The blue-eyed man looked smilingly at a red-faced Mayyada and said, "Congratulations. He must be a very lucky man!"

Ghazal helped her as she tried on the dress. She saw and felt the deep hollow scars on Mayyada's white skin.

Flogged skin does not heal, ever.

She didn't say a word, and neither did Mayyada. Their silence expressed a thousand and one feelings.

"Just look at your dazzling beauty; *subḥaan-il-khaaliq*"[18] said Ghazal in an attempt to lighten the heaviness of their hearts.

Mayyada smiled. She couldn't believe that she was the same woman as the one who stood across from her in the mirror. The built-in corset pushed up her breasts and emphasized their roundness. She touched their softness. Ghazal winked while Mayyada's smile turned into laughter as she felt more empowered than ever before.

Her femininity empowered her.

The white gown embodied every young woman's dream and held a promise of the fertile lands of marriage and motherhood. She thought of her mother's conversation with a neighbour a few days back comparing marriage to a watermelon, where one couldn't tell whether it is sweet or tasteless; she prayed and prayed for a sweet watermelon.

They continued on for hours with their adventure, hopping from one store to another like butterflies in a field of

---

[17] A *Sura* is a chapter of the Koran. There are 114 chapters in the Koran, each divided into verses.
[18] *Subḥaan-il-khaaliq* is Arabic for Praise the Creator (God).

flamboyant *Gerberas* [19]. They were living a dream.

But everything comes to an end, even dreams. Their short-lived dream was shattered into pieces as Mayyada met eye-to-eye with her brother Mohammed. Her niqab was lifted above her head, and there was nowhere to hide from her identity.

She was no longer able to feel her knees. The only words she recalled ringing in her ears, words that later haunted her in her daydreams and nightmares: "You prostitute. You whore. You cunt."

After Mayyada had fallen to the ground from the force of the slap on her face, he humiliatingly dragged her out by the arm with her body sweeping the floors of the mall and parking lot.

Once they had arrived home, he pulled her head cover off, ripped her *abaya* open, turned her on her stomach and began flogging her back with his belt.

Her mother was screaming and pleading for her son to stop. But he continued until he ran out of steam.

While being flogged, Mayyada felt the excruciating pain and wondered if this would affect her childbearing ability. Her only escape from the hell in which she lived was marriage, and no one would marry her if she were unable to bear children. She placed her hands on her belly hoping to armour her femininity.

He pulled her by the hair and threatened, "I swear on our God that I will kill you before you disgrace our name."

As his arms gave in, he began to kick her with his boots, blindly, until his legs too grew weak and tired.

---

[19] *Gerberas* is a plant of the daisy family with large, flamboyant and brightly coloured flowers.

"I hate him," she said to Reem." I am safe from him in this prison."

She rearranged the sweater she wore on her head. They had stripped off her *hijab* [20] before shoving her into the prison cell, and her only head cover was the sweater she wore. She felt stripped to the bone without some sort of cover on her hair.

"What brought you here?" asked Reem.

"I walked in a demonstration," replied Mayyada. "And you?"

"My posts on Facebook."

"Oh, that should not be too bad of a sentence then," Mayyada said with certainty.

However, her words were of no comfort to Reem as she knew the severity of the insults that she had expressed accusing the president of being a war criminal, a mass murderer, and a butcher.

She had received a telephone call that morning and was asked to show up at the Security Branch before noon or else they would come and drag her from her home by the hair to the office, they declared. That was the extent of the message, with no other explanation whatsoever. She immediately guessed her offense; she also knew there was no escape. She walked herself to her doom. She did not tell her mother, but her father cried as he helplessly let her go. Nothing could have been done. Upon arrival, she turned in her ID, her watch, her purse, and was pulled by the hair into the prison cell.

---

[20] *Hijab* is a veil that covers the hair on the head of a female worn by some Muslim women.

They sat together with their backs leaning on one another for support, and the two lamented on Syria for hours in the darkness of their cells, the same darkness that had penetrated into the lives and hearts of every Syrian. All of the destruction, the spilt blood, their imprisonment, and the utter chaos—all of it sprang from a simple dream for a life of dignity and the most basic of human rights. But the dream was suffocated upon its birth. The Syria whose minarets and church bells echoed one another's call to prayer is the same Syria being destroyed in the name of a country by some, and in the name of a God by others.

"To be honest, I am questioning everything, Mayyada!" confessed Reem, "At least Syrians were alive and living life in the old days. At least there was no bloodshed. Today we are living because we have been spared death! "My cousin lives in *Idlib* [21]," said Reem, "Pre-revolution, she was an art teacher. But ever since Islamists entered and plagued the city, she is no longer permitted to teach art, barber shops are closed as men are now to grow their hair and beards, jeans are taboo for they are a Western product designed by pagans, men are patrolling the streets during the months of Ramadan to make certain that no one is cooking, and...." She was silent for a few moments and then exclaimed, "You know, I truly believe that religious hell on Earth is far worse than hell itself!"

Reem, like Mayyada, was also a Sunni Muslim, but her family was considered quite liberal in their style of life. They

---

[21]   *Idlib* is a city in north-western Syria. It has become an area of conflict between the Syrian Army and the armed factions that have taken over sections of the rural area of the province as well as some areas within the province.

did not cover their hair and wore the latest Western fashions showing off their tanned skin. Her father recited the Koran every day, but he never forced his daughter to wear the *hijab*. He always said that religion was never to be imposed on anyone, and that religion dwelt in the hearts of people and was reflected in their acts, and not by their dress. He also said that the paths to God are many.

Reem lived a considerably free life compared to some of her other friends. She was an emerging poet and had been invited to recite her poetry on many different occasions, during which she had the opportunity to meet a number of poets, including Nizar Qabbani and the Palestinian Mahmoud Darwish. One of her favourite encounters was with the Syrian poet Adonis.

She had held his words of poetry as sacred as those in the Koran. Only a week ago, prior to her imprisonment, she had posted his words on Facebook:

> I see among the battered books
>   under the yellow dome punctured city flying.
> I see walls made of silk sheets and
>   a murdered star swimming in a green vessel.
> I see a statue made of tears, of the clay of limbs—
>   and prostration at the feet of a king. ᶠ

She thought of her beloved Syria, a Syria that has been brought to kneel at the feet of kings in crowns of diamonds and gold and of presidents with white smiles wearing flamboyant-coloured neckties. Her country, the mother of all countries, was now pleading mercy at the feet of a cold-hearted callous fate. Syria is a mother who has had to witness her sons and daughters aiming weapons at one another, shooting in the name of a country, and slaughtering and beheading, before her own eyes and the eyes of the world, in the name of a god.

The door was forced open, and once again, the soldier pulled her off the ground by the hair and shoved her in front of him. What was it about men pulling women's hair, she thought to herself. Was it a form of degradation and another way to exercise their power?

She found herself standing in front of a man who rested his large buttocks at the edge of a desk. He was wearing a green suit with badges and stars decorating his shoulders, sleeves, and front pocket.

He looked into her kohl-lined [22] eyes and smiled. She was an attractive young woman. Her friends envied her for her natural beauty and long black eyelashes. On an ordinary day, she only wore a bit of lip gloss. She believed that the secret to perfect skin was the laurel handmade soap that was delivered to her as a regular present from her cousin who lives in Aleppo's neighbouring Idlib.

"Facebook, huh? This is your offense. Do you plead guilty or not guilty, my beautiful?" he snickered while his filthy, blood-stained fingers intrusively crawled into her hair and felt a scalp that had only been touched by the fingers of her mother and her lover.

She felt his words creeping underneath her skin, penetrating to the bone. She tried to ignore the violent pounding

---

[22] *Kohl* is an ancient eye cosmetic. It is widely used in South Asia, the Middle East, North Africa, the Horn of Africa, and parts of West Africa as eyeliner.

at the walls of her heart and prayed to a watching God that this man does not hear it.

"I wrote every letter of every word," she said, looking him straight in the eyes.

He sneered. "So, I see that my little bad girl needs some discipline here," he said slowly approaching her. He stood eye to eye with her, a few millimeters from the tip of her nose. She could smell the smoke in his breath as he spoke to her. She continued to look directly into his eyes, unflinching, despite the pleas of her terrified heart.

She felt his two hands crawling onto her hips pushing her body closer to his.

She spat in his face.

He stood in shock, but she was even more shocked than he was.

He violently pushed her away. She felt the pain of the push in her tender breasts. He then called for the guard as he wiped the spit from his face, "Take this whore and discipline her."

The room was dark with a bright light projected at the prisoners. Two women awaited in the chamber. They tied her hands to a rope that hung from the ceiling, ripped her shirt off, and left her hanging in her black bra with her white skin exposed for what seemed like years.

She felt excruciating pain in her arms, even before the torture had begun. Her stretched muscles were aching severely.

A voice came from behind. Amidst the smoke, she could see the face of a woman, also with a green army suit and badges,

"Did you change your mind about anything ḥabeebty?"

"Never."

"Okay, very well. I gave you a chance. No one is to blame but yourself," she announced coldly with the eyes of a hunter musing over her prey.

And the torture began. As she felt the whip lashing the rawness of her skin, she thought of the people who had dreamed up torture methods and of the ones executing those fantasies: the pulling out of fingernails, burning of cigarettes on human flesh, flogging on naked skin, and on and on.

She recalled a conversation she once had with one of her friends who was taken to the Tadmor Prison [23] in the 80s and was underground for seventeen days. He narrated to her the details of the torture he had to endure. She remembered how she kissed the cigarette scars on his arms. Some of the scars were hidden to the naked eye underneath the thickness of the black hairs on his chest, but her lips followed his fingers as she felt and kissed each and every burn, wishing that her kisses could soothe a pain that would continue to ache until the end of time.

Worst of all, as he had explained to her, was the drowning method of torture where his head was forced under water for extended periods of time until he went blue and limp.

[23] *Tadmor Prison* is located in Tadmor (Arabic for Palmyra) in the deserts of eastern Syria, approximately 200 km northeast of Damascus. The structure was built as military barracks by the French Mandate forces, and today the Prison is known for harsh conditions, extensive human rights abuse, and torture.

The burning sensation of the leather whip was unbearable, she thought, but she immediately changed her mind as she felt the scorching metal rod on her body. She could smell her skin burning. She screamed. She thought of Adonis' words, of the splattered blood of the Syrian children, of the destruction, and of the cold refugee tents. Her pain was alleviated when contrasted to the images that flashed in her mind, but only for a few moments until the rod touched her skin again.

She began to cry.

In the other cell, Mayyada recognized Reem's voice as it pierced through the cold and callous prison walls. She felt the raw, deafening screams lashing her own bleeding heart. She covered her ears with her hands, and she cried and she prayed.

Mayyada was released three months later. Soon after, she was helped by her friend Ghazal to cross the Syrian border to Lebanon. Her niqab was a blessing in disguise as it concealed her identity until she arrived in Beirut. She now works as a caregiver for an elderly Lebanese woman. She no longer wears the niqab but covers her hair, loosely, with silky flamboyant headscarves to match her eyes, while allowing her black hair to fall on her shoulders and cover the eternal scars on her body.

Reem endured a total of six months in prison. She discovered that worse than drowning was rape. The man with the army suit, stars and badges, raped her twice a month. After her release, she sought refuge at her cousin's home in Paris and continues to defiantly write on Facebook. She has also created a non-profit organization that sends aid to Syrian refugees.

Mayyada and Reem have not crossed paths since their imprisonment, but the two continue to dream of reuniting one day again in a free Syria.

Alatrash

Story 3

LAMA

Alatrash

an excerpt from *The Prophet*
On Children

Khalil Gibran G

Your children are not your children.
They are the sons and daughters of Life's longing for
    itself.
They come through you but not from you,
    and though they are with you,
      yet they belong not to you.
You may give them your love but not your thoughts.
For they have their own thoughts.
You may house their bodies but not their souls,
for their souls dwell in the house of tomorrow,
    which you cannot visit, not even in your dreams.
You may strive to be like them,
    but seek not to make them like you.
For life goes not backward nor tarries with yesterday.

Alatrash

LAMA

"Ugh! Life isn't fair! You're so lucky to have an open-minded mother," said Layla [24] in an enviously cynical tone, "But such is the way of the world—you're born into wherever the hell fate decides to throw you. Some land on their feet, and some, bam, flat on their faces, and they ain't got a choice but to get up off their faces and walk."

Lama [25] had always contemplated Layla's words. Yes, the world is truly an ironic place and impossible to understand. Perhaps her grandmother's explanation was the only thing that had ever made sense to her.

Everything in this world made perfect sense to her grandmother. She would explain, as per the teachings of the Druze faith, that as the body dies, every soul is reincarnated into another life and another body, and through the successive reincarnations, the soul is able to experience different lives under different circumstances. She referred to this as divine justice, which, she explained, also yields divine mercy where a soul is given more than one chance for their actions and spiritual journeys.

"Indeed, God (Holy is his name) is fair, ḥabeebty; life is more than fair," she would say, placidly, with a peace of mind

---

[24] *Layla* is a feminine name and it is Arabic for Nocturnal; of the night; nightly.

[25] *Lama* is Arabic for The Darkening of the Inner Part of the Lip. It is a noun used as a feminine name.

that dwells only in the minds of believers.

Lama loved her grandmother's visits. She came to stay with them for 6 months and then would go and visit her son's family in Halifax for the other six months of the year. It was always a countdown to the day she left. The grandchildren loved the warmth, the stories, and the cooking that came along with the visits. Lama's mother and uncle considered their mother's presence in their lives an honour bestowed upon them by a generous fate. Many of their friends lived thousands of miles apart from their mothers, and Lama's family were eternally grateful for their mother's presence in their lives.

No one knew as many stories as Lama's grandmother. She was an anthology of short stories. Every evening, she heated the water on the stove in a silver kettle and arranged the tools for drinking *maté* [26]—an elegant mate gourd [27] with a silver rim and a gold and silver engraved metal straw. On the same tray there were three small elegant silver and gold containers—one filled with maté, the other with sugar, and one left empty for rinsing the straw with hot water and sanitizing it, as it was shared by everyone in the room. She also liked to use a lemon peel to sanitize the straw. Drinking maté with Lama's grandmother was cultural protocol and a ceremony. It stirred memories of the past and awakened endless tales awaiting to be told.

Her grandmother's maté was the best she tasted because

---

[26] *Mate*, also known as yerba maté in the west, is a traditional Middle Eastern, and South American, infused tea. Syria and Lebanon are the largest maté importers (in the Middle East) of mate from South America.

[27] A *gourd* is a hollowed and dried squash plant used as a vessel for drinking maté.

it contained an extra generous amount of cardamom. Lama would first breath in the aroma of the cardamom before sipping the hot water.

Her favourite tales were those on reincarnation. They were fascinating stories. "Your cousin, Riyad, was born screaming at the top of his lungs." Her grandmother would always use this same story as an introduction to the topic, "No one and nothing could soothe him since birth. They drugged him with anise so that he could sleep and let his poor mother sleep."

The white *Fouta* [28] covering her grandmother's hair never seemed to be arranged to her liking. Every five minutes or so, she would loosen it, re-tuck the stubborn pieces of her hair underneath the white fabric, and then reposition it to cover her chin with the excess of white fabric hanging on her chest; she looked like a saint.

"As Riyad grew older", she continued, "he began to recall flashes of his past life, and it all made sense after. He was the reincarnated soul of a young man who had died in a car accident at 32, leaving his wife and three children behind. Riyad was obviously not ready to depart from his past life and so he was born crying and grieving his loss. His pain was immense".

"Riyad is an explanation of why some of us are born with sadness and sorrow. Then there are those who are born with a smile on their faces. Why? Because their souls had lived a fulfilled previous life, likely long enough to see their grand-

---

[28] *Fouta* is a traditional head-cover worn by some Druze women. It is made of thin white cotton or linen fabric.

children, like I have seen you *tiqibreeni* [29], and had died at peace as they left their tired bodies and were reincarnated as babies cradled in their new mothers' arms."

The stories would continue for hours and so did the passing of the maté gourd.

Lama was grateful for her current station in life. She was blessed to have been born in Canada to a mother who had decided to see the world, not only through one set of lenses but with all shades of colours, and through the eyes of all people in humanity. Um [30] Lama had always taught her daughter to present herself as a Syrian-Canadian, expressing with patriotism, "Your soul *ya* [31] Lama is of Syrian heritage and your heart blossomed in the land of the maple leaf. You are not one or the other but a perfect amalgam of the two, the East and West combined, and I wish for you the perfect balance of the two."

Balanced, she was. In her university, Lama was the President of the Syrian-Canadian Association and took pride in

---

[29]   In Arabic, the literal meaning for *Tiqibreeni* is May You Bury Me. However, it is used as a term of endearment where one wishes that they are buried by their loved ones instead of outliving them.

[30]   *Um* is Arabic for Mother of. Um Lama is Arabic for Mother of Lama where it is the norm to call parents "mother of" and "father of" (Abu) their oldest born son. In this case, Lama did not have a brother, hence her name was substituted in.

[31]   *Ya* is a vocative particle used before the person being addressed.

building bridges between East and West. Her favourite activity was to screen movies in which peaceful and unifying messages were expressed through the arts.

"What are your plans for the evening? Can Kristian lend you for a night, perhaps?" asked Layla in a tone that was charged with envy.

"We are watching 'Four O'clock at Paradise' [32] tonight; we are going to screen it next month. Join us, would you?" invited Lama, wholeheartedly, with a smile that showed the whiteness of her teeth against the redness of her lipstick.

"I'll pass. Always something political! Poor Kristian! If you decide to watch something with the actor Ashton Kutcher, then give me a call," winked Layla.

"Okay, Ashton Kutcher is next, I promise—I like the fact that he played a role for our Syrian-blooded Steve Jobs," said Lama with a mischievous wink.

"*Wallah* [33] you're crazy! Now even Kutcher is a part of your political agenda! Poor Kristian," said Layla laughingly. She was known on campus for her laugh; it was the kind of laugh that shook grounded rock out of its place.

He noticed everyone's head turning as she walked into the room. She was strikingly stunning. She looked like she had

---

[32] *Four O'clock at Paradise* is a post-revolutionary film produced by Syrian Mohamad Abdulaziz.
[33] *Wallah* is Arabic for By God.

walked out of the pages of One Thousand and One Nights [34]. Her exotic long black hair took his breath away. He was very proud to be with her. She carried the entirety of Middle-Eastern charm on her long black eyelashes.

They embraced. He was over six feet tall and blonde, with a South African heritage, and his embrace was big and warm. Each time he hugged her, he lifted her off the ground and kissed her on her lips, pouring his endless passion into her heart.

She felt secure with him. He was five years older than she was. His career in journalism took him to the darkest corners of the world and added another 100 years to his age. There was something very beautiful about being with a man who was older and wiser. Men of many years knew how to treat and how to love a woman.

His travels filled him with worldly wisdom and down-to-earth humility. He lived alongside the poorest people in Cambodia, the hungriest in Somalia, and the saddest in Syrian refugee camps.

He took her hand and kissed her, "How have you been? I've missed you." He ran his fingers through her hair. "I wish I could travel in the blackness of your hair for centuries."

"Who wrote that, Nizar Qabbani?" she asked smilingly.

"No, Kristian Lang," he smiled.

---

[34] *One Thousand and One Nights* is a collection of Middle Eastern and South Asian stories and folk tales, of uncertain dates and authorship, compiled in Arabic during the Islamic Golden Age. It is also known in English as The Arabian Nights, *Alf laylah wa laylah.*

Between them were a thousand and one stories.
Between them there were Arabian deserts and African Safaris.
Between them was cardamom Arabic coffee and Rooibos [35] tea.
Between them was Asmahan [H] and Laurika Rauch [I].
Between them was a day of absence and a burning longing.
Between them were amorous whispers and passionate kisses.
Between them were sleepless nights under the light of a moon that shone on all.

They finished their coffee and headed home to watch Four O'clock at Paradise. She loved that he was passionate about her causes. Their passion for making a difference in humanity and for building bridges and connecting people brought her closer in mind and spirit to him than with anyone she had met before. Their blood lineage was different, their souls born on different continents, but their dream was one, and as they embraced, they too became one.

There is something also beautiful about being with people

---

[35] *Rooibos*, meaning "red bush", is a broom-like member of the legume family of plants growing in South Africa's Fynbos region. The leaves are used to make an herbal tea called rooibos or bush tea (especially in Southern Africa) or sometimes redbush tea (especially in England).

different than ourselves for they help us to better discover ourselves. Kristian and Lama were different and one at the same time.

As they watched the film, she thought of the darkness that had overcome Syria, and of the divisiveness caused in the name of a God and in the name of a country. The movie explored the lives of seven people whose fates intersected on the same day in a Damascus that was swinging between life, death, and becoming a legend.

What a pity! So many divisions and so many walls, she thought to herself.

There were even rock-ribbed walls tenaciously erected within her life, even in the midst of the unfenced Canadian landscape; they were cultural walls that deemed a Westerner different from an Easterner and a Canadian from Syrian.

Immigrants, for example, feared mixing within their new environments. Traditionally, the worst nightmares for immigrants were intercultural marriages for they wholeheartedly believed that their native cultures would melt away in the process. They could not see beauty in the fusion of blends, colourfulness in the multicultural mosaic, or refinement in evolution.

Lama understood the phobias of immigrants as they felt the threat of the new culture enveloping their own and threatening to erase their identity in a foreign land. But she also felt the struggle of second-generation immigrant children, ones who were torn apart as they were yanked from one side to another, from their present and familiar lives to practices and convictions from an abstract past that existed in a world very far away from their own.

She held his hand and placed it on her heart. She loved him more than life and thanked a fate that was more than generous to her. She was aware of the envy of her Syrian girlfriends. She was almost afraid of their envious eyes and prayed that her reality would last for eternity.

As the movie came to an end, he wiped away her tears.

She felt his fingers on her neck, andante, slowly, as if they were playing a piano.

She had always loved the feeling of someone's fingers on her skin—it numbed her senses. She remembered her grandmother's fingers caressing her forehead as she recited Arabic prayers. Lama was never certain of the effect of her grandmother's prayers, but she nevertheless loved the feeling. It was soothing.

But Kristian's fingers were magical. They did not numb her but instead awakened every cell of her femininity.

His lips followed in the track of his fingers, and as she felt their wetness on her skin, she closed her eyes and surrendered, sinking into his sea of pleasure.

"I want to make love to you, Lama."

"But," she said while he gently placed his fingers on her lips, whispering softly in her ears the words of Omar Khayyám ᴶ, "Dead yesterdays and unborn tomorrows, why fret about it, if today be sweet."

She smiled. She thought of how much she loved him. She contemplated his words. All they had for certain was the moment, the now. Lama was never convinced of what was preached on the permissible and tabooed. Rubáiyát of Omar Khayyám were her holy scriptures. She and Kristian had been memorizing his lines of wisdom. She thought of his words:

Poor soul, you will never know anything
   of real importance. You will not uncover
   even one of life's secrets.
Although all religions promise paradise,
   take care to create your own
   paradise here and now on earth.

She turned her face towards Kristian. He brushed her hair back behind her ears, removed her silver earrings and put them next to the vase of red roses, and began to gently kiss the corners of her lips. Their redness tasted sweeter than the sweetest of South African wine.

"Lama," he loved to pronounce her Arabic name.

"Kristian," she echoed. She yearned for him.

His fingers were gentle. A fire of passion was ignited as his lips travelled her female geography, her mountains and valleys, looking for fountains and streams from which to quench his thirst.

The feeling of her naked skin against his was intoxicating. There were no layers to separate them. They were two hearts stripped to raw passion. Time froze. There seemed to be no one in the world but him and her.

Her body was a rich terrain whose pores smelled of the aroma of all flowers combined. It was the scent of a woman, and it was sweeter than Sandalwood incense and more fragrant than the Viktor & Rolf perfume she wore.

Her words gradually transformed into moans, and it was on their wings that he travelled into her paradise, a paradise with rivers of milk and honey.

He put her fingers in between his, stretched her arms above her head, and slowly began to kiss the back of her arms, tasting every inch of her white skin, while their bodies danced in perfect harmony to the rhythm of her moans.

They wished that this melody would never end. As they danced, he whispered in her ears,

Love is not an Eastern tale
in which the hero and heroine are married at the end,
but it is sailing the sea without a ship
and feeling that reaching our destination
is impossible. ᴷ

Lama wondered if others also made love to poetry. Making love to poetry gave birth to a euphoric sensation that condensed One Thousand and One Nights of love into one.

He was like rain falling in June.

She breathed in the moment and felt rain showers of magical dew, mixed with stardust, quench the thirsty grounds of her paradise.

She wished her rain showers on Layla, on every Syrian and South African, and on the fertile grounds of every woman in this universe.

Everything ends, even dreams. [36]

It seems as if fate cannot stand to see happiness last. Why is it that something as beautiful as Lama and Kristian's love could not last forever?

Fate snatched Kristian from Lama's hands after a two-year battle with cancer. It broke her heart, but it did not succeed in stealing the memories of their love, ones that will defiantly continue to live until the end of eternity.

Lama believed, deep down in her heart, that Kristian must have been born crying in the arms of his new mother, grieving their loss of one another.

---

[36] This line is from the Lebanese singer Fayruz (also spelt Fairuz, or Fairouz meaning *turquoise* in Arabic). Born Nouhad Wadi Haddad in 1934, she is one of the most widely admired and deeply respected living singers in the Arab world. Her songs are constantly heard throughout the region.

Alatrash

Story 4

UM JAAD

Um ³⁷ Muhannad

Ghada Alatrash ᴸ

5 a. m.
The first day of exams
at the University of Aleppo.
She prepares breakfast
for her son Muhannad
who stayed up
until 2:00 a. m.
studying to the light of a candle
for his architecture exam;

the electricity was out yet again.
She brews his coffee
with extra cardamom
and two overfull teaspoons of sugar—
very sweet,
just like him.
She prepares mint tea,
just in case.
By 5 a. m.

---

37 Many Syrian women are nicknamed "mother of " their
firstborn son. Hence, *Um Muhannad* is Arabic for Mother of
Muhannad.

On the table is
a bowl of her homemade *labneh* [38]
with olive oil and dry mint sprinkled on top,
a plate of cucumbers
the reddest tomatoes she could find,
a bowl of green and black olives with
pieces of lemon and stems of thyme,
her hand-made pickled *makdous* [39]
and *Saaj* [40] bread she baked this week.
She doesn't have eggs
but *Um Nabil* (the neighbour)
will deliver some later today.
Tomorrow, she will scramble them
with parsley and onions,
just as he likes them
for there is always tomorrow.

---

[38] *Labneh* is Arabic for condensed yogurt that is used as a spread
on pita bread or as a dip.
[39] *Makdous* is Arabic for eggplant.
[40] *Saaj* is Arabic for an inverted iron bowl, like a dome,
traditionally used for baking bread.

5 a. m.
"It's five *habeeby*
Your coffee is ready
and so is your breakfast."

She doesn't eat
but watches his hands
as they move from one plate to another
to the light of a candle.
He holds her two hands,
kisses them one by one,
and says
'Yumma habeebty' [41]
pray for me.
I will be back by 5 *inshallah* [42]

1 p. m.
Two Explosions.
1 p. m. – 3 p. m.
Um Muhannad praying
to an Allah deafened
by the noise of praying mothers.

---

[41] *Yumma habeebty* is Arabic for My Beloved Mom.
[42] *Inshallah* is Arabic for God willing.

3 p. m.
Banging at the door;
Um Nabil
weeping
wailing
howling
pulling her hair
screaming:
"They bombed the University of Aleppo's Faculty of
    Architecture;
Muhannad,
Muhannad.
Muhannad."
5 p. m. :Muhannad...
6 p. m. 7 p. m. 8 p. m. 9 p. m. 10 p. m. 11 p. m. 12 a. m.
1 a. m. 2 a. m. 3 a. m.
4 a. m. : waiting.

5 a. m.
Breakfast is ready,
a plate of scrambled eggs.

Alatrash

UM JAAD

She decided that she would take the safest route. Her Canadian friends were not able to fathom her trip to Syria, a "warzone", but she had no other options. This trip was for the sake of her sister, Um Jaad [43].

Her trip began at Vancouver's International Airport and ended at the Rafic Hariri Airport in Lebanon. European airlines were no longer flying into Damascus as the city had been declared a war zone. Beirut and Amman became two detour options for travel to Syria.

She spent the night in Beirut and met with the taxi driver at 5 a. m. the next morning. Her sister had arranged for the driver to pick her up in Beirut and drive her to Homs.

The trip seemed endless, one road block after another guarded by young armed men asking the same questions at each stop: "Where are you coming from, where are you heading to, do you have anything to declare in your bags, how much cash do you have?" and so on.

She was used to such questions and interrogations at American borders while carrying a Syrian passport. But ever since she had become a Canadian citizen, she was no longer a potential terrorist nor a threat to U.S. national security!

9/11 laws decreed that Syrians are to be treated with great caution and scepticism. Yet what never made sense to

---

[43] *Jaad* is an Arabic adjective for diligent. It is also an adjective used as a masculine name in Arabic.

her was that there were no Syrian passengers on the planes that carried out the attacks.

While she felt the sadness and pain of the American people on that dark day in American history, she could not understand why Syria became part of the post-9/11 "axis of evil" list, especially since some nations were excluded from the list, and, unlike Syria, were up to their elbows with their involvement in the attack. Nevertheless, she had no choice but to abide by the American officers' commands and surrender her body to their intrusive searches.

Her Syrian passport was the source of both her pride and indignity all at once. Her feelings of frustration, helplessness and even hatred escalated each time she had to cross U.S. borders. Time after time, they forced her to stand with arms stretched out against a metal bar and legs spread apart, while an officer's fingers felt and violated every inch of her body, all because of the passport she carried. She recalled how she stood at the window and counted the number of cars welcomed onto U.S. soil simply because they were driven by Canadian passport holders. Even the cars were more fortunate than she was, she thought.

She had always wondered if Canadians truly understood the value of the passport they carried in their hands and if they realized that each one of them had literally won the lottery by having simply been born, by serendipity, on Canadian soil. She often contemplated this question: Did Canadians truly understand the value of the brand name stamped on their passports, and moreover, did they realize what others would pay for that label? The price for immigrants was heavy. It cost them a homeland, their families, and often leaving behind their own children.

Yet, today was more painful than anything she had experienced in her attempts to cross borders. Her own people interrogated her in her own homeland, in her native tongue, and on her native soil. For the first time in her life, she felt like a stranger in her homeland.

As she drove into Homs, she couldn't stop the tears from falling or her body from shaking. The taxi driver sympathized, "You must not have returned after the incidents." She shook her head for words were suffocated in her throat.

She looked out of the car window, devastated at what her eyes saw. The familiar neighbourhoods had now become ghost towns. She recalled her mother's constant complaints about the noises in the neighbourhoods and how they disturbed her afternoon nap. Once upon a short time, there used to be merchants roaming the streets and shouting, "Artichokes, eggplants, tomatoes, cucumbers," with crowds of people haggling over prices; there were children ringing their bicycle bells, music blasting in the shops, young men racing on motorcycles with their 80s leather jackets and slicked-back hair, and young women dressed in heels and tight blue jeans, giggling, swinging their hips as they walked the busy sidewalks and strolled the crowded shops. Today the silence was deafening. Homs had been strangled.

Cement buildings had collapsed like houses of cards. Faces of apartments were charred with missing balconies and walls. Cars were black, some half buried under the rubble and concrete. Everything looked dead. There was no sign of life.

In her home in Vancouver, she had hung a tapestry of Pablo Picasso's famous Guernica painting that he once painted in response to the bombing carried out by Germans and Italians on the Spanish village of Guernica. The painting depicted the tragedy of war and, in particular, the suffering inflicted on the Spanish people. The people in the image were not soldiers but innocent civilians. Today, the tapestry carried an even deeper meaning. It did not only tell of the Spanish tragedy, but also reflected the Syria that she was now seeing. In the painting was a woman grieving over a dead child in her arms with a wide-eyed bull standing over her head. Today, the image of the despairing woman happened to also represent her own sister, Um Jaad.

As they drove into her sister's neighbourhood, she saw a few people roaming the streets with weighted shoulders and long faces reflecting their heavy hearts.

One sign of life were the clothes hanging on lines on empty balconies. She thought of the days when her mother would point to the facing balconies and identify the neater housewife from the messy one by the way the clothes were arranged on the lines. She could even tell which housewife's whites were whiter than the others.

There was also a strict etiquette to be followed when it came to where to place specific clothing items. Under-garments, especially those that belonged to the females in a household, were to be placed on rows that were not exposed to other balconies or the street. She recalls how she once hung a bra on an outer line and was reprimanded by her mother for what seemed like hours. "Where is your brain? Could you not think for a moment about the neighbours seeing your red bra? Have I not taught you any manners? Where is your shame? How is this different than standing naked in front of everyone?"

In Syria, clotheslines are more than mere strings on which clothes hang—they are culture and tradition; they are etiquette; they carry a mother's scent and the aroma of laurel soap; they narrate all kinds of tales about next door neighbours and make known who's the tidier wife; they announce the arrival of a baby and whispers of wedding nights.

It was so very heart warming to reflect on those memories today. But she was grateful for her electrical drier in Vancouver. Clotheslines are not designed for a rainy Vancouver, and are a disappearing part of Canadian cuture or practice.

Her hands were shaking.

She knew that what lay behind the door was a very bitter reality. Her memories of the past were warm but her present was bleakly cold and barren.

She rang the doorbell. Her sister, Um Jaad, opened the door. The darkness of her soul was blacker than the clothes she wore. There was no colour to her face; it was a pale shade of white. They embraced while their sour tears burned the walls of their hearts. From within the sobs, one word was heard, "Jaad".

Jaad was her only son.

They cried for hours. To lose a child was fate's most cruel sentence. Children are the essence of life for a mother; they are the sunshine in a household, and a fate that steals them from a parent's embrace is but a sick, merciless, and murderous fate!

Um Jaad's sister also had a son and she knew what it was to be a mother. A month ago, her son developed a pulmonary infection and she spent 3 days with him at The Children's Hospital in Vancouver. She hated and despised hospitals. A hospital's visit was fate's way of teasing a mother, reminding her of how fragile and temporary life is, forcing her to stand face-to-face with all the possibilities that might be awaiting her.

She remembered one woman waiting in line who especially broke her heart. The woman was of East-Indian origin, carrying a wilted 7-year-old in her arms. There was a big Indian population in Vancouver, and like all other immigrants, they also left a homeland in hopes of a better life for their children.

The little boy's head rested on his mother's shoulder and his eyelids were shut, too weak to move. Her embrace was that of a mother horrified of a villainous fate, and the dark bags under her melancholic eyes narrated a history of hardships and sadness. She was wearing a thin, tight, washed-out turquoise blouse that exposed the outline of her saggy, worn-out breasts, ones that must have milked many children and had long ago retired from awaiting the pleasure that came with a man's stroke. The child in her arms was probably her youngest, for she looked liked she was well into her 50s. If the Arabic saying were true, the dearest child to a mother is the one absent until they return, the sick until they are better, or the youngest until they grow older. This East Indian child was a combination of youngest and sickest. The Arabic saying failed to mention a dead child, and how dear he or she must be to a mother's heart. It was suffocating to stand and imagine the possibilities of what might become of this little boy and his terrified mother.

After three long days at the hospital, Um Jaad's sister was finally back home. She thanked the heavens above for her son's recovery and kneeled on her knees, praying on behalf of all mothers of sick children in the world.

The morning of October 1, 2014 was no different than any other morning for Um Jaad. She finished ironing Jaad's blue uniform and orange school scarf and went into his room to wake him up. She felt the warmth of his body with her lips; it was a heavenly feeling. There was nothing more precious to her than the smell of his skin as it sweat under the covers. She slipped under the covers, wrapped her arms and legs around his little body and whispered in his ears, "Ḥabeeby, it's time to get up for school." He begged, "Please let me stay home today."

"But how are you going to be my doctor one day if you don't go to school? Didn't you promise me that one day you will be my heart doctor and make sure that it's always happy?" Um Jaad asked with a mother's voice that was pregnant with hope.

She had prepared for him his *labneh* sandwich with dried mint and olive oil. He loved mint, and so she had planted mint in her flowerbed so that there were always fresh mint leaves to tuck into his sandwiches.

He pulled a letter out from the pocket of his pants and said, "It's for you, Mama. Open it." She unpeeled the many stickers he used to seal his envelope and read his words, "You are the best mother I have found. I love you Mama. I pray that God takes good care of you for me. I also pray that God takes care of Syria. Amen."

"Ḥabeeby! Amen," she kissed him on the forehead, carried

his backpack on her shoulder, and walked to school with his tiny hand in hers.

She thought of the God Jaad had prayed to. It seemed like God had recently been overcome by deafness, for Syrian prayers were not answered these days. Perhaps he was also overcome by blindness, for had he seen the red blood spilled on Syrian soil, surely he would have intervened. Or perhaps the epidemic was global, for not only the supernatural had gone deaf and blind, but also all of humanity, and they had even become mute for that matter. Her country's screams were ear piercing as it was being strangled and its children slaughtered. But more deafening than the screams was the silence of the world.

Um Jaad volunteered her time with the Red Crescent in Homs, and lived the pain of the atrocities that were slowly erasing Syrians off the map. She prayed that no harm would reach her Jaad, and hoped that her good deeds would turn into karma that would protect her son.

"I love you, ḥabeeby. What do you want to eat after school today?" she asked.

"Spaghetti," he answered with a smile that showed a missing tooth and another peeking out halfway.

She kissed him goodbye. Each time he left the house, she felt stripped of her heart, to the bone, especially these days.

A few hours later.
A blast.
Windows shattered.
Red tomato sauce.
Spaghetti noodles.
Screams.
Sirens.
Glass.
Backpacks.
Children's drawings.
Blood.
Body parts.
A child's leg.
A dead child.
A dead teacher.
Chaos.
Chaos.
Chaos.
A dead child in a man's arms.
Jaad. Jaad.

This happens to be the doom of many mothers in Syria today, awaiting the help of a desensitized, deaf, and mute humanity. Jaad is one of the hundreds of thousands of Syrians killed since the crisis began in March of 2011.

Alatrash

Story 5

H.ANAAN
&
SALAAM

Alatrash

an excerpt from

And We Love Life

Mahmoud Darwish [M]

...and we steal from the silkworm a thread
to build a sky, and to fence in this departure.
And we open the garden gate for the jasmine
to go out into the streets...

Alatrash

H. ANAAN
&
SALAAM

"Ḥanaan [44], I am not physically attracted to women," he
said as he cried bitter tears. "I don't know what to do with
myself and who to turn to. I could never share this with mom
and dad. I can't take this pain any more."

His crying was more like a wailing. There was nothing
more unsettling and heartbreaking than the sound of wailing.
It was usually women who wailed. The worst wailing Ḥanaan
had heard in her lifetime was at her grandmother's funeral in
Syria. She recalled how her coffin was placed in the centre of
a great big room. Chairs were placed in rows facing the
coffin. Everyone from the village had gathered to pay their
condolences at the funeral. *Suras* from the Koran hung in
golden frames on the aged walls whose cracks resembled the
wrinkles on the faces of dead bodies in coffins. The sour
stench of death filled the place.

The funeral was very different from the ones Ḥanaan had
attended at churches and funeral homes in her hometown of
Fort Worth, Texas. Wailing was not a part of Western funerals.

---

[44]   *Ḥanaan* is Arabic for Affection, love, soft-heartedness. It is also
a noun used as a feminine name.

Only solemn funeral hymns echoed in the church, silencing visitors and sending them into a reflective state of meditation. Syrian funerals seemed sadder.

In a Syrian funeral, people were separated into two different rooms, one with men and another with women. Regardless of whether or not it was part of their religious practice, women wore some sort of cover on their hair, as it was a sign of paying respect. The family of the deceased always sat closest to the coffin, some crying silently, and others weeping. At times the wailing voices were so shrill that they not only pierced the hearts of those present but must have also cut through the soul of the deceased.

During her grandmother's funeral, Ḥanaan remembers how her five aunts took turns expressing lament and saying statements like, "Oh mother, you are going to be so missed. What will we do without your presence amongst us?", "You lived a queen and you died a queen, oh mother," and "You were the crown of our household, mother." In between, there were also moments of silence where one could only hear sounds of moaning mixed with phrases, "Ya-immee",[45] "Immee-Ya-Immee." Then, all of a sudden, one of the daughters would have an urge to speak again, and wail and weep, and give voice to the sadness of her broken heart.

To hear a woman wailing was distressing, and at times deafening, but to hear a man wailing was excruciatingly painful. She kissed her brother's cheek and tasted life's bitterness in his tears. His confession was not a surprising piece of news for her as she had always suspected that her brother was homosexual. Yet, she had always hoped, and

---

[45] *Immee* is colloquial Arabic for My Mother. *Ya* is a vocative particle used before the person being addressed.

even prayed every night, that it was only a passing phase.

She felt the heaviness of the weight placed on her shoulders. There was nowhere to turn or seek advice. Her Christian friends in Fort Worth were as closed-minded on the issue as her Middle Eastern family and friends.

Theoretically, she and her brother lived in what was considered an open-minded American society that embraced people of all colours, backgrounds and sexual orientation. But reality was different. Perhaps homosexuals were not publicly flogged in U.S. streets, but they were certainly looked at by many as different or even abnormal. Within the borders of the Texan Christian community in which she lived, some even considered them un-Christian and hell-bound.

If such news were to reach her family in Syria, it would be catastrophic. It would destroy her parents' reputation, shredding it to pieces, and would unforgivably and eternally scar her parents' names.

She thought of the wrinkles on her father's face and the calluses on her mother's hands—wrinkles and calluses that embodied years of sacrifice and hardship. Her parents had sacrificed a homeland for a better future for their children. They migrated from Syria to the U.S. in the 80s hoping to provide their children with the security and new horizons that were promised. They asked for nothing in return but to see their son and daughter successful and happy.

She began to cry. She couldn't bear facing the sadness and disappointment of her beloved parents.

"Oh Baasil [46]," she said in a broken voice.

The two sobbed in an embrace.

---

[46] *Baasil* is Arabic for Brave. It is also used as a *masculine name.*

"His name is Ḥazem [47]. He is a Law student. He is my best friend, Ḥanaan, and my soul mate," said Baasil, pulling out his deepest secret from underneath the rubble of a shattered heart.

He gently wiped the warm tears from her face, "To come to terms with my identity ya Ḥanaan was a journey that took many years to complete. I have travelled into the deepest and most hidden corners of my soul. I crossed terrains that were flooded with tears. Many nights I would awaken drenched in pools of sweat and tears. But the tears were cleansing and healing. They washed off the lies and dissolved all the layers. I feel stripped to the bone, but I have never felt as true, my beautiful Ḥanaan."

"If I could have chosen another way, believe me I would have. No one in their right mind would choose to walk this grueling, arduous road by choice. I have no choice, Ḥanaan. This is who I am and how I was born. But I also deserve to live and find my happiness."

Ḥazem's name flashed on the screen of his phone. He asked Ḥanaan if she would like to meet him. She nodded.

"Hello ḥabeeby Ḥazem. Can we meet at al-*Saaj* [48] downtown? Ḥanaan will be joining us."

---

[47] *Ḥazem* is Arabic for Resolute. Ḥazem is also used as a masculine name.

[48] *Saaj* in this sense is the name of a restaurant.

A waitress approached them with a wide smile and said in her Syrian Arabic, "Baasil and Ḥazem! It's been a while! How are you two?"

"We're fine, Zeina [49]. This is my sister Ḥanaan," said Baasil holding his sister's hand.

"*Ahla w sahla* [50], Ḥanaan. *Nawwartee* [51] our place," welcomed the waitress.

It was clear that the waitress had not only known Baasil and Ḥazem, but also welcomed them as regulars at her restaurant. It was heart warming to know that there were people like Zeina who exercised no judgment. Zeina was also Syrian, and most likely was raised in a society that deemed homosexuality a taboo. However, she had clearly freed herself from the shackles and chains imposed by the archaic narrative of society and culture.

What did it take for Zeina to cross over the bridge, Ḥanaan wondered.

One of Ḥanaan's closest friends, Anna, was of Dutch origin. Anna's brother, Hans, too, was homosexual. Ḥanaan had accompanied Anna to visit Hans in Seattle during their Spring Break vacation the previous year. It was her first close personal encounter with an openly homosexual man.

Hans lived in an apartment in downtown Seattle. Ḥanaan recalls thinking of Hans' home as one of the most elegant she had ever visited. It was small, but every corner was styled

---

[49] *Zeina* is Arabic for Beautiful. It is also used as a feminine name.
[50] *Ahla w sahla* is Arabic for Welcome, in colloquial pronunciation.
[51] *Nawwartee* is Arabic for You Lit Up (feminine), in its colloquial pronunciation. It is used here to express that the visitor lit up the place with her presence.

with grace, reflection and sophistication. On the walls, he had framed large photos of prominent leaders of our world including Nelson Mandela, Mahatma Gandhi, and Martin Luther King. Under Mandela, an inscription read:

No one is born hating another person because of the colour of his skin, or his background, or his religion. People must learn to hate, and if they can learn to hate, they can be taught to love, for love comes more naturally to the human heart than its opposite. [52]

Under Gandhi's photo were these words,

First they ignore you, then they laugh at you, then they fight you, then you win. [53]

Under Martin Luther King's photo was this quote:

We must accept finite disappointment, but never lose infinite hope. [54]

There was depth to Hans' home. No matter where one turned, there was meaning and a mirror for internal reflection.

Hans noticed Ḥanaan admiring a row of graceful white, yellow, and pink orchids that lived happily at the window of his kitchen. "I love my orchids. They symbolize beauty, exoti-

---

[52] Nelson Mandela, South Africa, 1918 - 2013, from *Long Walk to Freedom.*
[53] Mahatma Gandhi, India, 1869 – 1948, (but also attributed to American trade union leader Nicholas Klein)
[54] Martin Luther King , America 1929 – 1968.

cism, and delicacy. They are also said to symbolize love," he said smilingly. "What's your favourite flower, Ḥanaan?"

"Jasmines. White Jasmines," and she added, "They carry the scent of Damascus in their fragrance; they grow in Syrians' hearts and the scent lingers on their fingers."

She thought of Hans. He was a man who could feel. Perhaps his journey to discover his identity awakened every dormant cell in his body and brought him to unearth, touch, and feel the true meaning of life, one that is much deeper than the surface on which most of us seem to live.

Yet when it came to her culture, things were different. Journeys had boundaries and the horizons were limited, some no higher than the ceiling of one's home. There were no grey borders. Everything was either engraved with bold black letters or in scarlet red. The black was acceptable. The red was unacceptable, off limits, unthinkable, and taboo. Homosexuality happened to one of the more intolerable taboos. Perhaps it was accepted as a norm of life in foreign cultures, but within the walls of one's home, it was catastrophic.

The three ordered Arabic coffee. Ḥazem declared with excitement, "I have news, Baasil! Our application to adopt a Syrian child has been approved. We are about to welcome a little Syrian girl into our lives. I will buy her plane ticket tonight."

They informed Ḥanaan of what they had long been working on in secret. More than a year ago, they had submitted their application to adopt an orphaned Syrian child, and today, final approval was granted.

Ḥanaan could not find the words to describe what she felt—admiration, joy, and pride. At that moment, tears were her only form of expression. Goodness still existed in the world. Hope was alive and it was embodied in the souls of these two men with whom she sat.

Throughout life, she had been taught that the likes of Ḥazem and Baasil are cursed with a disease, sick, and bound for hell. An ironic world indeed, she thought to herself. Those fighting, killing, beheading and raping in the name of a God were bound to heaven and awarded virgin brides, while two men like Ḥazem and Baasil, who were the manifestation of goodness and the essence of truth, were deemed pagans destined to burn in God's scorching fires.

She smiled at the two truly beautiful men with whom she sat, asking, "May I join the two of you at the airport when the time comes?".

Ḥazem held her hand, placed it on his heart, and all three cried in an embrace.

"What's your name, ḥabeebty?" asked Ḥanaan in Arabic.

"Salaam [55]", the little girl whispered in a shy voice.

She had brown curly hair. The curls were dark brown at the roots and leisurely became lighter until they were golden at their ends. Her green eyes were outlined by the blackness of her long and dense eyelashes. They were glassy and expressionless. They reflected the horrors she had witnessed.

The female U.S. immigration officer handed a red carry-on bag to the three of them as she smilingly caressed one of Salaam's curls. One could see that behind the dark navy suit,

---

[55] *Salaam* is Arabic for Peace. It is also used for both a masculine or feminine name.

stars, and badges, was a mother's heart pulsating with sadness and heartache. "Take good care of her. The world needs more people like you," she said and left them before the tears surfaced in her eyes.

Salaam was holding in her tiny hands a red teddy bear. She also carried a yellow blanket for her bear with the word Love sown in English letters. Around her neck, she wore a gold necklace with an eye pendent. The pupil of the eye was blue and the lid was embroidered with white cubic zirconia. Culturally, the charm of an eye symbolized a shield of armour protecting its owner from any "envious" eyes encountered in their life's journey. It was common to see people wearing eyes as charms on chains, bracelets, or at times, pinned to a baby's shirt sleeves. But the magical powers of Salaam's charm were obviously obsolete. The charm had clearly done a very poor job in protecting little Salaam whose life was far from magic.

"How old are you ḥabeebty?"

"Eight," she whispered shyly in Arabic.

"My name is Ḥanaan, and this is Ḥazem and Baasil."

She nodded submissively surrendering to a fate that she did not trust any longer, a fate that had stolen her father, her mother, her brothers and sister, and her childhood. She was a survivor of the Ḥoula Massacre that took place on May 25, 2012 in a cluster of villages north of Homs. According to UN statistics, 108 people were murdered on that day, including 34 women and 49 children. Of these 108 massacred was Salaam's father; of the 34 women, was Salaam's mother; and of the 49 children, were Salaam's two brothers and one sister.

They placed the McDonald's Happy Meal on the table in front of her and invited her to eat. She examined the red carton box with the bright yellow smile drawn on it and slowly pulled out its contents: a cheeseburger, French fries in a red carton pouch with the letter M also in bright yellow, a yogurt tube, apple wedges, and a miniature Barbie doll. Upon seeing the doll, her face lit up. She caressed its soft blonde hair and admired its fancy pink dress with her tiny fingers. But her smile slowly faded away as she looked up and said with a soft broken voice in Arabic, "I wish I could show this to my sister."

Salaam's words hung in the air.

Her sister was sprayed with bullets after being shoved into a room, as was the fate of every member of her family. Salaam came back from the neighbour's home to find the bloodstained bodies of her family lying dead on the grey cement. She had been stripped of everything she had ever loved, and the pain had perforated her bones.

Everyone remained silent for they knew that no reply could comfort Salaam's broken heart. She went back to admiring the doll, began to braid her golden hair, and as she did, her body rocked back and forth.

"I'll name her *Amal* [56]. That was my sister's name," she said in Arabic.

Ḥanaan held Salaam's little shivering hands and kissed her on the forehead. She was grateful for Ḥazem and Baasil who were true manifestations of hope in a dark humanity.

She wiped away Salaam's warm tears, but the pain she could not.

---

[56] *Amal* is Arabic for Hope. It is also a noun used as a feminine or masculine name in Arabic.

And what has happened to Salaam?

For the first few months, the last word heard from Salaam was her sister's name "Amal". She went into a state of silence for weeks and weeks.

Ḥanaan accompanied Salaam to every counselling session. Salaam's heart was never whole again. Reality is that fragments of her heart will forever remain buried in that mass grave in Houla.

Today she speaks fluent English, but she continues to cry in her sleep and wakes up screaming. She has adapted to her new environment, as is the case with children, but even as she smiles, there is a sadness in her eyes.

Baasil's father did not speak to him at first, but gradually came to accept the situation. His only request was to keep the news secret from family and friends in Syria, as it would cause eternal disgrace to the family's name. His mother, like all mothers, swallowed the pain for the sake of her son, despite its sour bitterness.

Baasil, Ḥazem, and Ḥanaan became the father, mother, brothers and sister for Salaam, and their love was fate's way of compensating for Salaam's pain.

Alatrash

Story 6

WARD

an excerpt from *The Prophet*

On Marriage

Khalil Gibran [N]

Then Almitra spoke again and said, 'And what of
  Marriage, master?
And he answered saying:
You were born together, and together you shall be
  forevermore.
You shall be together when white wings of death scatter
  your days.
Aye, you shall be together even in the silent memory of
  God.
But let there be spaces in your togetherness,
And let the winds of the heavens dance between you.
Love one another but make not a bond of love:
Let it rather be a moving sea between the shores of your
  souls.
Fill each other's cup but drink not from one cup.
Give one another of your bread but eat not from the
  same loaf.
Sing and dance together and be joyous, but let each one
  of you be alone,
Even as the strings of a lute are alone though they quiver
  with the same music.

Give your hearts, but not into each other's keeping.
For only the hand of Life can contain your hearts.
And stand together, yet not too near together:
For the pillars of the temple stand apart,
And the oak tree and the cypress grow not in each
    other's shadow.

Alatrash

WARD

"Ḥabeebty Ward [57]... It has been 30 years since the day you left Damascus on that hot August afternoon, heading to the land of the 'broad stripes and bright stars... the land of the free and home of the brave'."

It was also thirty years ago, on that same day, that my heart was shattered into a million pieces. I have thought of you each and every day of those thirty years, ceaselessly.

I learned of your engagement twenty years ago and of your marriage. I am very proud of your accomplishments as a writer, and I have read every word ever written by you. They are engraved on my heart. I know all about the Americas because of you, of their tolerance, freedoms and 'endless horizons'. Your writing has shortened the distances and soothed my pain. It was a window through which I could catch glimpses of your world, and a tunnel through which my heart secretly visited yours.

I am closer to you than you know, Ward.

Ward... I love you with no hopes or desires, and I am writing to also wish you a happy birthday. — Yours, Taym [58]".

Ward felt her heart skip a few beats as her eyes scanned his words in her Facebook inbox. She reread them, this time

---

[57] *Ward* is Arabic for Roses; flowers; blossoms; bloom. It is also a noun used for both feminine and masculine names.

[58] *Taym* is a masculine name that stems from the Arabic verb *Tuyima* means To Become Enthralled by Love, to be Captivated by Love.

savouring every word. She breathed in their aromas of incense and perfumes. They were intoxicatingly delicious; they were like drops of rain falling on her dry heart and quenching its thirst. She felt eighteen at forty. She remembered Taym, the neighbour's boy who lived next door to her childhood home in Damascus.

She thought of Damascus—a most enchanting city, home of the Umayyad Mosque [59], where the cooing of white doves echoed by the mosaic walls was more magical than the best concerts she had heard in Carnegie Hall. She thought of Qasioun Mountain [60], of its cafés vibrating with young lovers on romantic escapades and bustling with their love-smitten energy. Her favourite café was *Aḥla Ṭalleh* [61]; it sat on the shoulders of the mountain overlooking a charm that only dwelt in the folds of the oldest city of the world. Damascus was the mother of all cities.

She thought of her own mother. She wished she were a little girl again, holding her mother's hand and accompanying her on shopping escapades and social visits. Her favourite

---

[59] The *Umayyad Mosque* of Damascus is located in the old city of Damascus and is one of the largest and oldest mosques in the world. After the Arab conquest of Damascus in 634, a legend dating to the 6th Century holds that the building contains the head of John the Baptist, a prophet honoured by Christians and Muslims alike. The mosque is also believed by Muslims to be the place where Jesus will return at the End of Days.

[60] *Qasioun Mountain* is a mountain overlooking the city of Damascus. Its highest point is 1,515 metres (3,776 ft).

[61] *Aḥla Ṭalleh* is Arabic for The Best View. It is also a name of a café that sits on the shoulder of Qasioun Mountain in Damascus.

outing of all was to the Turkish Baths (*hammams* [62]). It was there, leaning against the stones of the walls, hundreds of years old, where she had first discovered the many hidden secrets of womanhood.

She closed her eyes and felt an intense nostalgia. She envisioned the mosaic-tiled walls that held on their shoulders the ageless domes for centuries. She could feel the warmth of the hot steam and the numbing sensation of the massages, and she smiled at the heartening memory of the sight of naked women whispering, giggling, laughing, and enjoying sheer and unrestricted self-indulgence. They were women of all ages and sizes; the spirit of the place was drenched in passion and the air drunken with love.

The women scrubbed one another's bodies, vaunting the softness and silkiness of their skins. Nudity was only to be practiced on wedding nights and in bedrooms within the institute of marriage. A Turkish *Ḥammam* was one other place in which a woman was allowed to expose her nudity and boast her femininity without any reservations and without the scrutinizing eyes of a man. It was an exercise of freedom where she could strip down to the skin, no layers; it was a celebration of womanhood, of a God-given exhilarating femininity, and it was delightfully liberating!

---

[62] *Ḥammam* is Arabic for Bathhouse. An old legendary story says that Damascus once had 365 *hammams* (or Turkish baths), one for each day of the year. The *Ḥammams* in Damascus date back to the 12th century CE. Today, fewer than 20 Damascene working *hammams* had survived modernization.

She reflected back on her childhood with Taym. She wished she could reach into her computer screen, collect his words, and scatter them in the garden of her heart. Her heart was shrouded with shrubs and thorns, and she longed for roses and jasmines.

She recalled her visit in the spring to the Butchart Gardens in Victoria [63] and yearned for the spectacle of blushing Camellias, rosy Magnolias, white Daffodils, pink Cherry trees, and the endless fields of the red, orange, yellow, green, blue and violet tulips.

It is true that a woman resembles a flower, for a woman is as beautiful and her essence is as fragrant. Like flowers, women have their own colours, textures and scents. They are the most delicate of creations and require the gentlest of touches. The more love they are fed, the more magnificent their bloom. And also like a ripened flower in her full bloom, a woman is most beautiful in the prime of her life. Ward was a woman in full bloom.

Her fruit was ripe, in full splendour, but without anyone to feel, reap, taste and savour its sublime magnificence.

---

[63] The *Butchart Gardens* is a National Historic Site in Canada located near Victoria, British Columbia on Vancouver Island. They boast a group of floral gardens that receive close to a million visitors a year.

What harm was there in replying to his message, she thought to herself; perhaps words were the magic fertilizer that would transform her infertile heart into the garden of flowers and roses she craved. Her heart was barren like a dry desert, and she could no longer bear the thirst and hunger, especially when within her reach was a fruit no less seductive than the forbidden fruit in Adam and Eve's hands. She, like Eve, was also human.

Time was impatient, and its train was leaving with or without her. If she didn't choose to leave, she would end up staying, and she did not want to stay.

The snow was falling on the Rocky Mountain peaks in the distance. She listened to Fayruz ° singing,

September, with its yellow leaves,
made of gold, outside of windows,
reminded me of you.

She looked through her window onto the ever-greenness of Colourado's cedars, pines and firs. She envied the trees for their eternal youth and beauty. Perhaps there was beauty to everything, green or yellow, for as the saying goes, *beauty is in the eye of the beholder.*

She was awakened from her dream by a memory that came knocking on the doors of her heart.

She turned to her screen and typed, "Do you remember the Jasmine tree that climbed out of our balcony and onto the front gate entrance of our building in Damascus? And do you remember the bouquet of Jasmine that you plucked and gave me as I returned home from school one afternoon?"

She hit the send button...

"I remember the jasmine, and I remember every detail about you. I live on those memories, Ward. I want to hear your voice again," he replied.

She was curious to hear the sound of his laughter. She thought about the different laughs of the people in her life, and how they were a true reflection of one's personality. At times, they even reflected the size of a person's heart.

"Ward," he whispered hoarsely.

"Taym" she replied with a smile he couldn't see. He laughed. His laugh was a thunder that awakened her dormant heart. His voice was an electrical wave that travelled through the distances and awakened every cell of her womanhood. And her voice transformed his feelings of longing into utter craziness.

Minutes of silence stood between the two. She was trying to understand how his voice sounded so very familiar and close to her heart. How could he feel so close? Had their souls been conspiring behind their backs and bringing them closer than their minds were able to understand?

"I have a thousand and one questions for you, Ward. But most important, is life treating you kindly?"

"I can't complain, Taym. Fate has been generous to me, although not always kind," she replied with a choked smile.

"And you Taym. How are you?" she asked.

"I am fine now, Ward. With the sound of your voice all my dreams are now fulfilled, and my only wish at this moment is for this conversation to never end." He sighed, "For the past thirty years, Ward, I have dreamt day and night of living this moment with you."

She smiled and he felt her contagious smile. "Tell me about you." she curiously asked.

"I was married," he answered, "to a French woman after immigrating to Sweden. We were married for 5 years, and then we parted ways. She is a friend now. Ever since the beginning of our relationship, she suggested that we live in separate homes. As a Middle Eastern man, I rejected this notion and called it westernized modern nonsense. Looking back, I think she might have been much wiser than the Middle Eastern in me."

Ward also happened to believe that marriage is a failed institution, with only a few exceptions as is the case with everything in life. She saw marriage as a process in which two separate trees are uprooted from their soils and planted in one another's, with the expectation that they can grow in each other's shade. Naturally, one, if not both trees, would wither, and at times, one might even die in the process. Only in exceptional cases, when trees are carefully planted within a healthy distance from one another, can they both blossom; distance provides space for personal growth.

But she had also come to accept that the world would continue to function robotically with respect to marriages—with their effervescent wedding ceremonies, promises, toasts, and delusional fantasies—and unions would be made on this strange place called Earth, until the end of time, simply because that's just the way things go.

She thought of her husband and of how their marriage had become stale over the years. It had no pulse. Day after day, their paths grew in separate directions. Gradually, their marriage fell prey to the poisonous fangs of routine and remained under its deadly grip until it went into a permanent state of paralysis accompanied by complete loss of feelings.

The wall that was separating his soul and hers grew taller than the wall erected in Palestine. It was more impenetrable and much darker. It was not grey, but black, where no memories and no words could be painted on its sides, and where no light, no sun, and no warmth penetrated either.

Her state of balance was always perturbed by their encounters, ones that were more like intrusive storms that always left her like a dead log floating in a sea of tears and sadness. As the storm ended, she was left, each time, with less womanhood, whose most sacred of temples were destroyed and left in ruins.

She deeply believed that if married couples could have things their way, the majority of them would choose to simply leave after a few years of marriage.

Her soul was left cold for many years, and she was afraid that it had died.

But Taym's call was reassurance of the existence of remnants of life. She felt, for the first time in what seemed like a thousand years, that electrical wave travel through her body igniting excitement, daydreams and smiles that lit up her life.

She turned on the warm bathtub water. She hoped that a bath would wash the day's mud off her heart. Her girlfriends had given her a jar of bubble bath for her 40th birthday. She removed the crystal lid and poured the pink liquid into the hot water. The pinkness blossomed into happy bubbles with colours of the rainbow, flirtatious bubbles anxiously waiting to find their place on her soft naked skin. She carefully dipped in her toes so that she wouldn't disturb the short-lived life of the fragile bubbles, measured the temperature of the water, and then slowly surrendered to the numbing sensation of a hot bath.

She laid her head back and thought of him and of his phone call. She thought of life and of how it was ultimately as fragile and short-lived as the life of the bubbles on her skin. She longed to find love in her life, and she was acutely aware of her need. There was something peculiar about love and romance, she thought to herself. She had come to the conclusion that the secret to a happy romance was balance. She learned about the art of balance in a class she had once attended on Buddhism. In Buddhism, balance was referred to as the "Central Way", "Middle Path", or "Middle Way." Buddha used this concept to describe the character of the path he discovered leading to freedom and liberation. It implied a balanced approach to life and the controlling of one's impulses and behaviours. Aristotle also spoke of a similar concept called the "Golden Mean" whereby, as per his teachings, it was the desirable centre between two extremes. It was the middle grounds between excess and deficiency. In his view, for example, courage is a virtue, but when taken to excess, it yielded recklessness, and when deficient, it became cowardice. The same was in relationships, Ward thought, for too much love is smothering and too little is negligence.

She scooped the steaming water with her hands, felt its streamlets seeping through her lazy fingers and trickling on her sedated bare breasts.

The messages and phone calls became candles that lit up Ward's life. His words were red embers that inflamed her ashen heart. They were the dew that washed away the pain of her yesterdays. Each word of each conversation was a step closer to him, melodiously bringing them to complete one another. She felt in her veins the birth of a new woman.

She looked for Marcel Khalifeh's name on her iPod and clicked on his song "The Most Beautiful Love". She closed her eyes and listened,

> Like grass that grows
> in between rocks,
> we were two strangers
> who found one another.
> …
> I love you like
> Travellers in a desert love an oasis of grass and water
> and like a hungry man loves a loaf of bread.
> Like grass growing in between rocks,
> we found one another,
> and we will remain friends everlastingly.[P]

"Where were you long before, Taym?" she asked after a few months of phone calls and conversations. He was silent for a few moments and then cleared his throat and began to sing Fayruz's words. She smiled at the sound of his voice,

> I wish I could have reached out my hands
> and stole you from them,
> but because you are theirs,
> I took back my hands and I left you my beloved. [Q]

"May I see you, Ward?" asked Taym with a confidence she lacked.

"See me?"

"In a country of our choice with no desires other than to live a moment that might not be present tomorrow." He sat silent for a moment and then said, "Ward, do you know what has been more painful than longing? It is the pain of longing for the impossible, which only yields more longing... It is the emptiness that comes with embracing a dream."

She looked at a quote from Eckhart Tolle [R] that she had framed and placed next to her computer: "Life is the dancer and you are the dance."

She realized that she was about to embark on a new path. But this path was not a new beginning. It was one that began at the last footstep she had reached on an arduous journey of life.

She thought of Damascus. But Damascus today was in no mood for lovers. The city's doves had stopped cooing and the white Jasmines were dressed in black, mourning the dead. Damascus' children were seeking refuge in all corners of the world, looking for a tent in which to cover their bare souls; there was no shelter for their shivering hearts.

She thought of Asmahan singing—

The intimate nights in Vienna
have breezes from paradise
and melodies in the air
that bring a bird to cry and sing.[5]

She longed to cry and to dance, to strip away the rusted layers, down to her rawest feelings, down to the bone.

"Vienna," she whispered.

She stood waiting nervously for his face to emerge from in between the many colours of faces. Their eyes finally met and their long-awaited tomorrow became their now. His long black eyelashes were wet with tears of longing and joy. She knew that he would not have shaven his beard on the plane. They embraced, body to body and soul to soul. She felt the black stubs on his unshaven face, and she indulged in the scent of his manliness.

Time froze.

Her presence awakened his masculinity. His scent awakened her femininity. Her dry rivers began to flow again.

A woman loves to be embraced.

He held her face in his two hands and said, "Nothing is more beautiful than your eyes, but your eyes."

As she rested her head on his chest, her heart danced in ecstasy to the rhythm of his heartbeat, and their heartbeats together became the melody to which his life and hers danced.

Ever since Vienna, Ward and Taym have been meeting in different cities around the world. Ward did not accept Taym's proposal of marriage as she believed that the monotonous routine of marriage would poison everything beautiful in their relationship. Their relationship was born by pure serendipity and she wanted nothing to take away from the excitement of the unplanned and the accidental.

The distance between them kept alive their longing for one another. Like strings of a lute, they were separate but also together as they quivered to make music and to make love.

Over the ten years, their love gave birth to a garden of exotic flowers in whose shade they lay together in an embrace each time they met.

Meanwhile, Damascus was awaiting their visit; their future smelled of jasmine.

Alatrash

Story 7

UM MARYAM

My Father and the Fig Tree

Naomi Shihab Nye [T]

For other fruits, my father was indifferent.
He'd point at the cherry trees and say,
"See those? I wish they were figs."
In the evening he sat by my bed
weaving folktales like vivid little scarves.
They always involved a fig tree.
Even when it didn't fit, he'd stick it in.
Once *Joha* [64] was walking down the road and he saw a
    fig tree.
Or, he tied his donkey to a fig tree and went to sleep.
Or, later when they caught and arrested him, his
    pockets were full of figs.

At age six I ate a dried fig and shrugged.
"That's not what I'm talking about!" he said,
"I'm talking about a fig straight from the earth—gift
    of Allah!
—on a branch so heavy it touches the ground.

---

[64] *Joha* is a trickster figure in Palestinian folk tales

I'm talking about picking the largest, fattest,
    sweetest fig
in the world and putting it in my mouth."
(Here he'd stop and close his eyes).

Years passed, we lived in many houses,
none had fig trees.

We had lima beans, zucchini, parsley, beets.
"Plant one!" my mother said.
but my father never did.
He tended garden half-heartedly, forgot to water,
let the okra get too big.
"What a dreamer he is. Look how many things he
    starts and doesn't finish."

The last time he moved, I got a phone call,
My father, in Arabic, chanting a song
I'd never heard. "What's that?"
He took me out back to the new yard.
There, in the middle of Dallas, Texas,
a tree with the largest, fattest,
sweetest figs in the world.
"It's a fig tree song!" he said,
plucking his fruits like ripe tokens,
emblems, assurance
of a world that was always his own.

Alatrash

UM MARYAM

She carried in her hands a bag full with stems of herbs—basil, mint, tarragon, thyme, and anything else her hands could grab from the garden before departing to the airport. She also cut off a shoot of white jasmine and a yellow one, and placed them in the same white bag. She wrapped the roots with wet paper towels so that they could survive the duration of the 40-hour trip they were about to embark upon.

"*Wallahi*, you are crazy. Who does this? We are going to the U.S. For God's sake, they have herbs in the U.S.!" complained Abu Maryam [65] in utter irritation, muttering under his breath, "May God give me patience!"

"Yes, but Maryam has always said that American fruits and herbs are tasteless when compared to ours. I don't want to eat tasteless herbs for the rest of my life." She said stubbornly while silent tears began to fall again caressing the wrinkles under her weary blood-shot eyes, "And what if we don't come back?"

---

[65] *Maryam* is the Aramaic name of Mary the mother of Jesus. Maryam is also the 19th Sura (chapter) of the Koran; the name appears 34 times in the Koran.

They had lived all their lives in the Al-Jdaydeh [66] district in Aleppo. They were born there, and so were their parents and grandparents. It was their home and safe haven. It was the ground on which they first met. It was where Um Maryam shyly spent her first wedding night next to Abu Maryam on the same bed and under the same roof. It was where their daughter Maryam was born. It was also where Um Maryam tended her garden wholeheartedly and planted jasmine, roses, rosemary bushes, radishes, zucchini, cucumbers, tomatoes, green onions, egg plants and all the herbs with which she cooked.

Abu Maryam and Um Maryam had insisted over the past few years to hold onto the very last thread of hope before having to leave, but the situation had become not only dangerous but also life threatening. Islamist extremists had injected fear into the hearts of Al-Jdaydeh's Christian community. The Islamic State deemed Christians "non-believers" and pagans; they were hell-bent on mass murdering everyone who stood in the way, and Christians were always one of their targets.

The air of the city hung heavy in the streets, and the sight of its bloodstained sidewalks was both nauseating and horrifying.

A few weeks prior to their decision to travel to their daughter's home in the U.S., Islamist extremists had kidnapped two Christian bishops. Christians began to fear that the

---

[66] *Al-Jdaydeh* is a historic neighbourhood of Aleppo, Syria, that dates back to the 14th century. It is considered one of Aleppo's Christian quarters and is home to the Armenian Gregorian Church, the Greek Orthodox, the Maronite and the Syriac churches. It is noted for its winding narrow alleys, richly decorated mansions and churches, and has become an area of significant cultural and historic interest for international visitors.

ethnic cleansing wave that had swallowed the lives of Iraqi Christians was now heading their way. They were stripped of hope. They didn't trust the world to intervene any longer; they had to flee for their lives.

"You will see! They are not going to allow your green grass to enter the U.S. at the borders," Abu Maryam said in a cynical tone, now hoping to lighten her spirit.

She didn't reply, but squeezed the cross she held in her hands and continued to pray, wholeheartedly, asking God, His Son and Virgin Maryam to soften the hearts of the American officers who were to decide the fate of her sacred herbs.

The plane was full with Syrians leaving their homeland. It was a Syrian Exodus. All international flights from Europe had cancelled their services to Damascus as the country had become a dangerous war zone. Lebanon was one country that had taken up flights between Damascus and Beirut, and from Beirut, passengers were then able to catch their connections to Europe and to other corners in the world.

They took their seats on the plane. Abu Maryam placed his black Samsonite on his lap, and with trembling fingers he managed to rotate its lock. He checked to see if everything was still in its place: a wooden cross engraved with the words *"Eli Eli lama sabachthani?"* [67], a photo of Jesus on the cross, an Arabic copy of the Holy Bible and another in English, an em-

---

[67] The verse appears in the *Holy Bible*, Matthew 27:46 and in Mark 15:34: "Around the ninth hour, Jesus shouted in a loud voice, saying *Eli Eli lama sabachthani?*" ('My God, my God, why have you forsaken me?).

broidered fabric purse with his wife's gold wedding jewelry wrapped in it, a bundle of U.S. dollars wrapped with a rubber band and placed in the zipper pocket, a folder with all of his land ownership certificates, a book of photos of the children, a brown bag for the grandchildren filled with Turkish delights of all flavours (rosewater, mastic, orange and lemon with sugar icing), and a book by Najat Abdul Samad titled, "Lands of Exile". Um Maryam only had one carry-on bag in her hand — the bag of herbs and jasmine.

He took out the book and closed the Samsonite briefcase, securing its lock again. He looked at the words on the cover of the book, "Lands of Exile". On the first page of the book, Najat wrote, addressing Syria,

Our pleas have become hoarse
Love us and put an end to our exile ᵛ

The exiled in her novel were those expelled to different corners of the Arab world, Europe and South America, but not to the United States. Abu Maryam and Um Maryam's names were now on the list of those expelled to the United States of America.

Abu Maryam contemplated for a moment the thought that he would one day send Najat a letter and share with her his U.S. experience so that she could perhaps write about it in her sequel.

To leave a homeland was to leave a piece of one's heart and soul behind. He cried as the plane departed the soil of his birthplace. He cried tears of pain; they were tears that sprung from a broken heart.

He closed his eyes and reflected on Palestinian Mahmoud Darwish's words:

You ask: What is the meaning of homeland
They will say: the house,
the mulberry tree,
the chicken coop,
the beehive,
the smell of bread,
and the first sky.
You ask: can a word of eight letters
be big enough for all of these components,
yet too small for us? ᵛ

The plane was bustling with noise and opinions, the loudest of which were the political ones. Politics had become the centre of all conversations, from dinner tables at home, to workplaces, and now onto planes. Many children were crying and the air was suffocating. All the passengers were Syrian, and everyone was on edge. There was no laughter; happiness was left behind, buried underneath the rubble and destruction in a war-torn homeland.

From amongst the crowd, the voice of a young man broke out in song. He was playing the *oud* [68] and singing Fayruz's song, "We will be returning, Oh love." He sang:

We will be returning, Oh love
we'll be returning.
Oh flower of the poor,
we'll be returning
on the fire of love...

---

[68]   *oud* is a form of lute or mandolin played principally in the Middle East.

we'll be returning.
We'll bid time farewell and
we'll tell time to forget us
on the land of forgetfulness...w

Within only a few moments, other passengers joined in song. Voices were mixed with tears. Children began clapping. A beautiful young woman, wearing a hijab with floral designs, lifted her arms and swayed her hands in the air while the tears streamed from underneath her closed eyelids. The stewardesses also clapped. The spirit of Syria filled the place.

Abu Maryam joined in song and Um Maryam cried as she clapped; others also cried for a wounded Syria that they were forced to leave behind, and that they did not wish to leave.

The flight took them via Beirut and London on to their final destination of Houston, Texas. Their daughter had lived in Houston for 8 years along with her husband and two children. Abu Maryam and Um Maryam had never visited the U.S. before. Their daughter had visited them in Aleppo every summer along with her children. They had not seen her since her last visit in the summer of 2011 after the revolution had begun in Syria.

For the past few years she had been begging them to consider moving to live with her in the U.S. It was more than heart wrenching for her to nervously anticipate the news every hour of the day while her parents lived on the burning grounds of a collapsing country. Time after time, she would hysterically run to the phone after hearing about a fired shell, praying that it had spared the roof of her parents' home. It was mental torture.

At first, Um Maryam and Abu Maryam rejected the idea of departure and escape. They couldn't imagine leaving. But with each passing day, their hopes diminished; and they had no choice but to pack their lives into their suitcases and leave.

An announcement was made asking all passengers to fill out their U.S. Customs Declaration Forms. Abu Maryam reached into his shirt's front pocket and pulled out his glasses and a Mont Blanc ballpoint pen. The pen was a gift given to him as a gesture of honour and appreciation in 2010 from the Association of Syrian Lawyers. His English was considered above average, but his accent was thick, with an Aleppo twang to it.

Learning languages was his hobby. He was always fascinated with how a language reflected the culture of its speakers. He had never met a native Spanish speaker but through learning Spanish, he understood the spirit of the people, and like Arabs, they were very passionate humans. He always smiled at how Spanish resembled Arabic in its exaggerated expressions—a simple English phrase like "my beloved" was expressed in endless ways in both Arabic and Spanish: "Miamor" (my love),"Mivida" (my life), "Mialma" (my soul), "Micorazon" (my heart); the corresponding Arabic was: "*Ḥabeeby*," "*Ḥayaaty*", "*Rouḥy*", and "*Qalbi*". The list was infinite. However, his daughter had told him that the Americans were "much more direct". She said, "No one goes around calling their beloveds *their heart*. They simply say it just as it is*: my love*". He believed that there was beauty to everything, the simple and the complicated, the direct and the passionate.

The customs form was short and simple, but answering its questions was painfully complicated, for the answers embodied a great loss, a tragic defeat, and shattered hopes.

He began to fill in the boxes:

1. Print your last (family) name. Print your first (given) name. Print the first letter of your middle name. Mikhail [69] Yusuf [70]

2. Print your date of birth in the appropriate day/month/year boxes. 17/ 04/ 1946 [71]

3. Print the number of family members traveling with you (do not include yourself). One: My wife.

4. Print your current street address in the United States. If you are staying at a hotel, include the hotel's name and street address. Print the city and the state in the appropriate boxes.
   3117 Over Street, Houston, Texas

5. Print the name of the country that issued your passport. Syria
   (Tears were falling as he wrote the answer.)

6. Print your passport number. 01889830

7. Print the name of the country where you currently live. Syria
   (His hands began to shake uncontrollably. As of that moment, his reality was that he had become homeless, without a homeland. The answer was only ink on paper and the realization was excruciatingly painful.)

8. Print the name of the country or countries that you visited on your trip prior to arriving to the United States. None

---

[69] *Mikhail* is a masculine name that comes from Hebrew origins. It means Who is Like God. In English, it is equivalent to Michael, Michelle, etc.

[70] *Yusuf* is a masculine name that is the Arabic equivalent to the English name Joseph.

[71] April 17, 1946 is Syria's independence day commemorating the evacuation of the last French soldier and Syria's proclamation of full independence at the end of the French mandate in Syria.

9. If traveling by airline, print the airline's name and flight number. If traveling by vessel (ship), print the vessel's name.
British Airways Flight 123

10. Mark an X in the Yes or No box. Are you traveling on a business (work-related) trip? No

11. Mark an X in the box. Are you bringing with you:
   a. Fruits, plants, food, or insects? Yes
   (He looked at the bag of herbs in Um Maryam's calloused hands. What would he have become without those hands?. They were sacred. He continued to cry.)

   b. Meats, animals, or animal/wildlife products? No
   c. Disease agents, cell cultures, or snails? No
   d. Soil or have you visited a farm/ranch/pasture
      outside the United States? Yes
   (He knew that the soil and the bag of herbs were destined for confiscation by the officers, and he was so very sad for another heartbreak that his wife was about to face, yet again. He loved her so very much.)

12. Mark an X in the Yes or No box. Have you or any family members traveling with you been in close proximity of (such as touching or handling) livestock outside the United States?
No

13. Mark an X in the Yes or No box. Are you or any family members traveling with you bringing $10,000 or more in U.S. dollars or foreign equivalent in any form into the United States?
No

Read definition of monetary instruments on ...

Thank you, and welcome to the United States.

The plane landed. After a journey that seemed like 100 years, they set foot on American soil. He was grateful for the U.S.. It was a second homeland for his daughter, the birthplace of his grandson and granddaughter, and a country that opened its doors to people of all colours and nationalities. Syria expelled its own children and watched them from afar as they begged for refuge in all corners of the world, some even thrown in cold and barren tents.

Not long ago, the word refugees represented the Palestinian people who had lost a homeland and were abandoned by all. Abu Maryam thought of the words of Mahmoud Darwish once again, while awaiting his turn in the immigration line:

The Earth is closing in on us
pushing us through the last passage
and we tear off our limbs to pass through.
The Earth is squeezing us.

I wish we were its wheat
so we could die and live again.
I wish the Earth was our mother
so she'd be kind to us.
. . .
Where should we go after the last frontiers?
Where should the birds fly after the last sky?
Where should the plants sleep after the last
    breath of air?
. . .
We will die here, here in the last passage.
Here and here our blood will plant its olive tree. [x]

He opened his eyes and looked at the people in line. They were of all colours—white, black, yellow and red. They were all welcomed on American soil, regardless of origin. Almost everyone who walked the streets in Syria was of Syrian origin. Indeed, it is a great country, this United States of America, he thought to himself.

Um Maryam was not thinking of poetry nor did she notice any of her surroundings. She stood with her cross squeezed very tightly in her hands and with only the white bag on her mind. She was reciting prayers under her breath. Abu Maryam could feel her heartbeat racing. He wished he could hold her; he could not remember when last he had held her. The years had dried up the tenderness in their marriage, and the war added layers of rust onto their broken hearts.

"Good evening. May I have your passports please?" said the American officer politely. The officer had a thick American accent, thought Abu Maryam. It was probably as thick as his English accent but with a Texan twang instead of an Aleppo one. The officer had blue eyes and blonde hair with a reddish tint to it. He looked very colourful, thought Abu Maryam.

"How was your trip?" he asked.

"Thank you, very well," answered Abu Maryam. Um Maryam stood silently, holding onto her white bag.

"What plants do you have, Sir?" the Officer asked.

"Yes, herbs in this white bag for my wife," he answered, "from our garden."

"I'm afraid you are not allowed to bring those into the U.S."

"Please Sir, my wife's heart has already been broken and you will break it into more pieces. Please sir. I guarantee that they are not contaminated."

"These are the rules Sir."

Abu Maryam looked at his wife and explained that she could not bring the bag into the country. She said in Arabic,

"Tell him that they are the only piece of our homeland that I brought with me. Tell him that they are its smell and taste, and I can't find this anywhere in the U.S."

The officer listened to her Arabic, understood the message through the broken tone of her voice, and shook his head, "I am very sorry Ma'am but this is the law."

Um Maryam, with tears flooding down her face, said in a broken English that she had neglected for years, "No. Please. Please. Look. I taste them for you." She put a few mint leaves in her mouth. Her tears were falling vigorously on her cheeks.

"For Jesus, the Son of God, let me. Please. I always pray for you. Please I may no visit my home country again, please. I have no home now. My home destroyed, my garden destroyed, my heart destroyed. I pray for your homeland America. I will plant this in my garden in Texas, and you come and visit me anytime. Please." Her tears sprung from a burnt heart and they also burned the officer's heart.

"Please, Ma'am. Stop crying. I am very sorry for your pain," said the officer as he closed the passports, stamped the date of entry—January 23, 2014—and said, "Welcome to the United States of America."

"*Abous-rouḥak* [72]," she cried.

---

[72] *Abous-rouḥak* is an endearing expression used especially in Aleppo (Syria), and it is applied in its figurative sense of the meaning. It is Arabic for I Am Kissing Your Soul; the female form is *Abous-rouḥik*.

Abu Maryam and Um Maryam live on the dream of returning to their beloved homeland of Syria. But until this dream comes true, both of them wake up every morning to their herbs and nourish their little garden in Houston, wholeheartedly. They continue to invite the neighbours to taste their Syrian dishes cooked with herbs from Syrian soil, while narrating stories about a homeland that awaits their return.

Um Maryam phones her neighbour in Syria on a weekly basis to check on her garden, and she dreams, day and night, of watering it once again with her own hands, and heart.

Alatrash

Alatrash

As Fayruz sang, "everything ends, even dreams" ...

and I will continue to dream. —GA

Alatrash

No More and No Less [73]

Mahmoud Darwish [Y]

I am a woman. No more and no less
I live my life as it is
thread by thread
and I spin my wool to wear, not
to complete Homer's story, or his sun.
And I see what I see
as it is, in its shape,
though I stare every once
in a while in its shade
to sense the pulse of defeat,
and I write tomorrow
on yesterday's sheets: there's no sound
other than echo.
I love the necessary vagueness in
what a night traveler says to the absence
of birds over the slopes of speech
and above the roofs of villages
I am a woman, no more and no less

The almond blossom sends me flying
in March, from my balcony,
in longing for what the faraway says:

---

[73] This poem represents me in every letter of every word.
—Ghada

"Touch me and I'll bring my horses to the water
    springs."
I cry for no clear reason, and I love you
as you are, not as a strut
nor in vain
and from my shoulders a morning rises onto you
and falls into you, when I embrace you, a night.
But I am neither one nor the other
no, I am not a sun or a moon
I am a woman, no more and no less

So be the Qyss[74] of longing,
if you wish. As for me
I like to be loved as I am
not as a colour photo
in the paper, or as an idea
composed in a poem amid the stags …
I hear Laila's[67] faraway scream
from the bedroom: Do not leave me
a prisoner of rhyme in the tribal nights
do not leave me to them as news …
I am a woman, no more and no less

I am who I am, as
you are who you are: you live in me
and I live in you, to and for you
I love the necessary clarity of our mutual puzzle

---

[74] *Qyss* or *Qays*, and Laila or Layla, are the lovers in the medieval
Arabic "virgin love story" Qays and Layla.

I am yours when I overflow the night
but I am not a land
or a journey
I am a woman, no more and no less

And I tire
from the moon's feminine cycle
and my guitar falls ill
string
by string
I am a woman,
no more
and no less!

Alatrash

Postscript

My identity is an amalgam of East and West. With that comes a very complex and often contradictory internal struggle. There is the Middle Eastern influence in me that has been engraved on the walls of my heart and then there is the Western influence that I have chosen to embrace with all my heart alongside my native Syrian identity. I am grateful for a fate that has allowed me the opportunity to be a hybrid outcome of both East and West.

I have always believed hybrids to be the most beautiful of products. However, in a cultural context, the hybrid can also be perceived with a negative connotation. Hybrids, in the eyes of some, are not purebloods and are inferior to the native race. Indeed, it's a pity how we humans, consciously, insistently, and persistently, continue to create divisions amongst ourselves, and, even more disturbing, we seem to find comfort and a sense of understanding in alienating one another. We mindfully allow these divisions to stand between us without any resistance, labeling us according to differences in nationality, religion, colour, and ideologies.

I write to try and make sense of all this.

In this book, I have documented short clips of Syrian women's lives. I can only speak of what I know and what I have witnessed, and I am writing with the hopes of beginning a new conversation: how beautiful it would be to eliminate borders and boundaries, to overcome cultural, societal, political, religious and ideological divisions—to plant the seeds of love in all hearts, and for all to reap the benefits of love.

To my children, I will do my very best to not impose any conditions, labels, or boundaries on your choices. I pray that you will soar to the infinite horizons, and that you will find and celebrate love when it comes your way.

Ghada Alatrash
March 2016

ghadaalatrash.me

Alatrash

Illustrations

Cover photo: David Salas / david-salas.com

Map, and Butterfly-Dream drawing:
  a Syrian friend who lives in exile today.

Flower icons from flaticon.com

Pomegranate	🌸
Watermelon	🌸
Passion	🌸
Laurel	🌸
Jasmine	🌸
Rose	🌸
Fig	🌿

Index of first lines

Alatrash

Literary endnotes

CPSIA information can be obtained at www.ICGtesting.com
Printed in the USA
LVOW11s2314240516

489838LV00001B/9/P